His laugh was low and mirthless. "If you think I wish to promote a romance between my brother and your sister, you are fair and far out. I came here out of boredom and chanced upon my brother once I arrived. He seemed as unhappy at seeing me here as you appeared to be to see him. And me," he added with a significant look in her direction.

"You can scarcely be surprised if I am not elated at the sight of you," Fiona said tartly.

This time his chuckle held some humor. "No, Fiona, I do not expect elation when you see me. It is an interesting concept to ponder, though," he added thoughtfully, "the picture of you smiling and greeting me agreeably. . . ."

Also by Rebecca Ashley
Published by Fawcett Books:

THE RIGHT SUITOR
A LADY'S LAMENT
A SUITABLE ARRANGEMENT
LADY FAIR

FEUDS
AND
FANTASIES

Rebecca Ashley

FAWCETT CREST • NEW YORK

FOR SPENCER WITH LOVE

A Fawcett Crest Book
Published by Ballantine Books
Copyright © 1990 by Lois Walker

Library of Congress Catalog Card Number: 90-93289

ISBN 0-449-21890-2

Manufactured in the United States of America

First Edition: January 1991

Prologue

As CHILDREN, Fiona and her brother Grove had played often with William. The three of them, along with Eliza, had run through the forest together and raced their ponies across the meadows. In the darkening woods they had told each other tales of horror until all were thoroughly frightened. It was twelve-year-old William and Grove who had carried Fiona back to the house after she fell into a ravine and wrenched her ankle.

But all that was in the past. Fiona had not spoken to William for nine years. Although their manor houses stood within a few miles of each other and one of his properties marched with her family's, she had steadfastly avoided him. Everyone knew of the trouble between the families. No hostess would invite both William and Fiona to the same soiree. Fortunately, William had spent little time in Surrey the past few years. He had been in London.

But now Fiona was in London for her sister Constance's Season, and there would be little chance of escaping the presence of the man she detested.

Chapter 1

"SHALL WE be going to church tomorrow?" Constance asked from the doorway of the dining room.

Fiona looked up from counting the silver and blinked in surprise. "You want to go to church on your second day in London?"

"Yes, I think we should, well—" the pretty young blond paused before concluding, "give thanks that we arrived safely from Surrey."

Fiona heard this in silence. It was not that she wished to discourage her younger sister's religious fervor. It was simply that she was startled by Constance's interest. Come to think of it, though, her sister had been showing more enthusiasm for their Sunday devotions in the last few weeks in Surrey.

"If you wish, of course we shall go. There is a church not three blocks from here."

"I want to go to St. Paul's," Constance said promptly.

Fiona was mystified but agreeable. "As you wish."

"Good." Her sister flitted from the room in a rustle of willow green skirts, her soft blond curls bobbing.

Fiona turned back to the work at hand. Checking the silver was one of the many numerous tasks that must be done in order to open a house that had been long closed. No one had used the spacious house just

1

off St. James's Square in nine years. Its rooms were still as lovely though, Fiona reflected as she wiped her hands on her apron and glanced around the dining room. The deep peach walls were unfaded and the holland covers had protected the cream-colored Louis XIV chairs well. With a bit of polishing, the silver epergne in the center of the long mahogany table would gleam. The wall sconces, too, would shine with a bit of attention from the servants.

Even more important than the house, though, was seeing that Constance have everything she needed to start the Season. That was why Fiona and her sister had come to London three weeks before the Season was to begin. Constance had complained there were many things she could not find in Surrey. She had heard of a linen draper in Mayfair in London who offered exquisite fabrics. Unless she wished to be completely démodé, she *must* buy her fabrics from him. Besides, in London, Constance had pointed out, she would be able to find just the right gloves and reticules and little satin slippers so that everything would be perfect for her presentation.

Fiona smiled to herself as she began putting the silver back into its chest. Constance need not worry so much about her clothes. With her delicate features and hair of spun silk, Fiona was certain Constance would not have the least problem attracting suitors. It was far more likely that Mrs. Dyer, the kindly chaperone hired to oversee Constance's presentation, would have her plump hands full with preventing gentlemen from becoming too forward in their attentions.

Fiona smiled as she thought how much her sister was going to enjoy her flirtations. What young girl did not want to capture a few hearts? During Fiona's own presentation nine years ago, she had not wanted for suitors. Even though dark-haired women had been the rage that Season and she so fair and blond, men had still paid court to her. She had received several offers and was in anticipation of more when her Season ended abruptly.

Fiona closed the lid to the silver chest with a quick snap and resolutely turned to an inventory of the candlesticks. She had far too much to do to waste time dredging up the past.

It mattered little how her Season had ended. It was Constance's that was important now. Fiona hoped her sister's natural beauty and charm would stand her in good stead and result in a brilliant match. She would hate for anything to mar Constance's Season as hers had been marred. But what could go wrong? Fiona asked herself reasonably. Constance was from a respectable family and came with a large dowry—Papa had left each of his three children amply provided for. Besides, Constance was sweet and behaved very prettily. In short, she had all the qualifications for a good wife.

Fiona was put forcibly in mind of her sister's charms the very next morning as she and Constance entered St. Paul's. Although the church was only half-full, it seemed that most of the gentlemen present glanced in their direction.

"See, you are already attracting notice," Fiona whispered to Constance as they started up the aisle.

"Some of them are looking at you," Constance whispered back. "You are not so old, you know."

"I'm seven-and-twenty," Fiona objected, but she was flattered all the same. She had grown accustomed to thinking of herself as a spinster, but that did not mean she disliked masculine attention.

Constance continued up the aisle beneath St. Paul's grand dome. Fiona reached for her sister's hand. "Where are you going? Could we not sit here in the middle?"

"I wish to be up close." The younger girl moved forward again, and Fiona had no choice but to follow. Her blue satin-striped redingote swept the floor of the vast cathedral. Feeling conspicuous as they continued up the aisle, she busied herself tucking a lock of hair back into her smart new bonnet. Just how far up were they going?

At home in Surrey the family had its own pew in the modest church. There Fiona expected to sit in the front, but not here amid the sophisticated, curious eyes of the ton who had arrived early for the Season.

Constance selected a seat three rows from the front, sat down with great aplomb and glanced around. Fiona sat beside her, stiff with self-consciousness.

Smiling, Constance leaned over to whisper, "We can hear better up here."

"We could have heard perfectly well further back."

"This is better," Constance assured her, folding her hands meekly on her lap and facing the front of the church.

The service started a short time later. They were in the midst of a hymn and Fiona was singing out strongly when she sensed her sister was preoccupied with other things.

She glanced over to discover her sister gazing to her left. Fiona could see just enough of Constance's profile to detect the coyest of smiles. Good heavens, the little minx was flirting with someone right here in church!

4

The song died on Fiona's lips as everything fell into place. This explained why Constance had been so intent on coming to St. Paul's and why she had selected a seat near the front. Constance had expected—perhaps even planned—to see someone here. Fiona looked around for the object of her sister's smile.

She was not long in finding it.

A man in a pew two rows across to the right was looking toward them. He wore a blue coat and white unmentionables. He was trim and athletic of build. His dark hair was short and his cravat flawlessly tied. The Honorable James Haversly. He was the younger brother of Lord William Haversly, eighth Earl of Haversly, Viscount of Wickford, and the detestable scoundrel who had shot Grove.

Blinking, Fiona turned to Constance in disbelief. Surely her sister would never encourage the notice of James Haversly. Constance's eyes were now lowered demurely but a trace of a smile still curved her lips upward, and she held her songbook with a daintier grace than was usual. She looked like a woman who knew she was being watched and who was enjoying it.

This was unconscionable. Fiona put a stern hand on Constance's arm and bent to whisper, "It would please me if you would attend to the service, my dear."

Constance's smile vanished. She looked down at the hymn and began to sing just as the last notes died away, leaving her momentarily singing alone in the huge church. She clamped her mouth shut and turned the bright red of a geranium.

Fiona was too distracted to concentrate on the rest of the service. How *could* Constance seek to attract the attention of James Haversly? Constance was well aware of the pain his family had caused their own family. Mama still could not bear to speak of her neighbors. Before Papa's death, he had a special road cut so he would not have to pass the Haversly's estate. He had forbidden his servants against any social intercourse with the Haversly's servants on pain of dismissal.

One thing was certain: Fiona was going to nip her sister's little affair in the bud. Once the service was over, she would have a talk with her sister. Meanwhile, because she was in church, she tried to focus on the spiritual.

As soon as she and Constance had entered the carriage, however, Fiona pulled off her bonnet and scorched a look across at her sister. "It appeared for all the world as if you were trying to start a flirtation with James Haversly. In church, no less. I pray you will tell me I did not see what I thought I saw."

Constance tugged at the wrists of her gray gloves and looked downward. "He happened to be there, and I nodded to him."

"It seemed to be much more than a nod," Fiona returned with spirit. "One would have thought you were casting out lures to him."

The younger girl looked up and met Fiona's gaze. "James Haversly is going to be here for the Season," she said in a voice full of reason. "You must have known when we came to London that we would see both him and his brother William at half the balls we attend. They are accepted everywhere, you know."

"I do not doubt we shall see them," Fiona agreed grimly. "London hostesses will not exclude them from their houses. Even hostesses in Surrey did not do that, although they never invited *us* to the same functions as the Haverslys. Some women will be misguidedly eager to have Lord Haversly in attendance for their "at homes" and parties. After all, he is a bachelor and a wealthy one at that. But either those hostesses can forget his past or they never knew of it. I, however, cannot possibly forget that William Haversly shot my brother."

During the silence that followed, Fiona felt certain Constance must be acknowledging the error of her ways.

Yet when her sister spoke again, it was to say in a very calm voice, "It has been so long ago, Fiona. Is it not time to forget what happened in the past?"

"Forget!" She almost choked on the word. "You were not there. You do not know what it was like to see Grove carried into the living room. He was ghostly white and bleeding horribly." Fiona felt a catch in her throat as she recalled that scene and the fear that had clutched at her. "Mama was beside herself with worry. Papa was furious. Lord Haversly was wise to flee the country, or I believe Papa would have killed him himself."

Constance tugged at her gloves again. "Grove did not die, though. He healed."

"Do you think that excuses what Lord Haversly did? Once Grove was well enough to talk, he told us Lord Haversly not only provoked the duel, he shot before Grove was ready. Duels are dreadful enough, but William Haversly acted completely without honor."

Fiona tried to temper her frustration with Constance by reminding herself her sister had been too young to realize how much Grove had changed since the injury. He was no longer the carefree, loving brother he had been. He had moved far from the family to live in the wilds of Cornwall. He seldom

7

visited and when he did, he seemed diffident and reserved. Mama's face always became gaunt with concern during those rare visits. For the loss of the old Grove, William Haversly was also to blame.

Fiona drew in a deep breath and said firmly, "What William did has forever divided our families. There can be no question of you forming an attachment for James Haversly."

After a silence and what Fiona thought was a sigh, the younger girl murmured. "I am sorry. I did not mean to overset you so."

Fiona patted Constance's hand. "I know you did not, dear."

During the rest of the journey home, Fiona was glad the affair had been put behind them. It was too painful to think back on it. It was doubly painful because Lord Haversly had once been a good friend to her and to Grove. Now she had nothing but contempt for him.

The three weeks until the Season opened passed quickly. In addition to shopping for fine kerseymeres and jonquil silks for Constance, Fiona had her own wardrobe to attend to.

Now that she was no longer a debutante, she was not limited by the pastels of youth and could indulge her love of colors. She bought yards of violet velvet and rose satin and filmy blue silk. The rich fabrics felt wickedly sensuous against her skin, and she loved running her fingers over the nap of the velvet.

Not that she had ever regretted choosing a quiet life with her family in Surrey, but it *was* exciting to be in London again. The glitter of the emporiums and the noisy pace of the city streets were heady. She had forgotten how much fun it could be to shop in bustling stores and to anticipate the round of parties.

Later in the Season, she would give a party for Constance. Already she had laid tentative plans for it, but first more preparation was needed on the house, and Constance must become comfortable and accepted in society.

Meanwhile, the sisters eagerly combed fashion plates, studied *Bell's Court and Fashionable Magazine addressed particularly to the Ladies* for hairstyles, and scanned the invitations that were already beginning to arrive.

On the evening of the first ball, Fiona's maid helped her into a high-waisted, rose-colored gown of fine muslin. Standing in her bare feet in the middle of the large room, Fiona stared across at the pier glass. The dress rested low on her shoulders, skimming just across the top of her bosom. She looked at herself critically as the Scottish maid made minor adjustments to the gown.

"You would not want to show too much, ma'am," the practical woman commented. "On the other hand, it does not hurt to let the gentlemen know you are a woman."

Fiona smiled. "I scarcely think it matters, Dorothea. Men will not notice me. Their attention will be fixed on the young girls being presented. Besides," she added with a shrug that caused the dress to slide downward provocatively, "I am not in the market for a husband."

"One never knows about matters of the heart," the maid murmured.

Smiling, Fiona ignored that. Writing and managing a household gave her plenty to do. Men seldom seemed worth the trouble they created. Of course she wanted Constance to have a husband. Young, innocent women like her sister needed a man's protection. But Fiona had learned to take care of herself.

"Sit down and we will make your hair beautiful."

Fiona sat patiently on the little velvet stool while the maid styled her hair into a froth of blond, then laced a beaded ribbon through the curls. Dorothea stepped back and nodded her approval. Fiona looked at her reflection and approved, too. The arrangement made her face look soft and young. A pretty glow suffused her cheeks.

At home she seldom took such pains with her appearance. She felt quite pretty as she stood, picked up her fan, and started out the door.

On the stairs she met Constance and Mrs. Dyer. Her sister was a vision in an ivory-colored frock with scallops around the neckline and hem. Her blue eyes were bright with the anticipation of her first evening in the swirl of London society. Fiona smiled gently at Constance's anticipation and recalled her own girlish enthusiasm for her first ball.

"Do I look all right?" Constance asked anxiously.

"You are lovely. Isn't she, Mrs. Dyer?" Fiona asked the thick-waisted woman in black who trailed behind them.

"Indeed she is."

"I hope you are right. There will be so many other young ladies there tonight, and I am certain they will all be beautiful. Is it hard to fix a man's attention?"

Fiona laughed. "You are asking the wrong person. I never married, so I obviously was not able to fix a man's attention."

As they walked out into the crisp night air, Constance objected. "I have heard you did not lack offers during your Season. It was only that you were too particular."

"I daresay I was too particular," Fiona agreed. She allowed the footman to hand her into the carriage and pulled her spreading skirts up after her. Mrs. Dyer sat down next to her. Pensively, she continued, "I should have been more willing to overlook a few faults."

"No, I think you were right," Constance said. The sidelights of the carriage cast a glow across her animated face. "No woman should accept a man who is not in every detail what she wants."

Fiona hesitated, sensing trouble in that way of thinking. "One must not be too exacting, my dear," she said carefully. "After all, having a husband and a home and a family are not things to be passed by lightly."

"You have done quite well without them, Fiona. You are happy."

"Yes, but my writing gives me great satisfaction. But you and I are different people. I do not think you would find my quiet life to your liking."

Constance shrugged and glanced away, her thoughts clearly straying to the evening ahead. "I hope I am asked to stand up at least once. It would be a shame if I were not after all those lessons with a dancing master."

Fiona laughed. "I wager you will be besieged with young men wanting to stand up with you."

"I hope so."

Fiona's prediction proved correct. They had been within the painted ballroom of Melbourne House less than two minutes before an officer Fiona knew from her own Season begged upon that acquaintance to gain an introduction to Constance. The pair were soon off dancing.

Mrs. Dyer went off to sit in the corner with three

other chaperones. Fiona spied Lady Eliza sitting across the room. She smiled and began making her way to the far side of the room to join her old friend. Now that Eliza was married and lived in Kent, Fiona seldom saw her.

"Hello, Eliza."

Eliza jumped up from a delicate settee to kiss Fiona on the cheek. "Dear, Fiona! I hoped you would be here this evening. Did you get my message that you must come visit? Do sit down. I'm here quite alone with nothing to do but look out over the dark park."

Fiona glanced toward the windows overlooking St. James's Park and then back to her friend. "Where is Harold?"

Lady Eliza made a wry face. "He has taken to the tables already." She spoke without any real concern, though. "Let us not talk about him. Tell me about little Constance. She must be very excited about her come-out?" Lady Eliza looked around. "Where is she?"

"There, in the ivory. Dancing with that handsome man in uniform."

Lady Eliza peered intently, then turned to Fiona. "Dear me. I had not noticed how very beautiful she has become. You will forgive me for saying she eclipses even you, and you were a diamond of the first water during your Season."

Sisterly pride overran any thought of jealousy. Gazing at Constance, Fiona said softly, "She is a lovely child, isn't she?"

"Indeed. She shall have no trouble at all making a suitable match."

"No."

"You must be very careful with her. These beauties are the hardest to manage, you know. Lord

Chesterman's second daughter, who was presented last Season, took the town by storm. Then she eloped with a coachman! Can you imagine? They were off to Gretna Green before anyone knew what they were about. It was shocking. Shocking." Lady Eliza repeated with relish.

Fiona laughed. "Dear me, Eliza. You sound as if you are living in anticipation of the next big scandal."

Her companion fluttered a painted silk fan and murmured with mock virtuousness. "Nothing of the sort, but one does like to be informed."

"I assure you Constance is a very levelheaded girl. She would never do anything so foolish as to run off with a coachman. In fact, she would not consider marriage at all without my approval." It was true that in the years that Grove had been gone and Mama ill, Constance had come to look to Fiona for guidance and advice.

"That is good." Lady Eliza put a gentle hand on Fiona's arm. "How is Grove?"

"He is well enough. He does not write often," Fiona confessed. Sadly, she went on to relate, "He is not the same cheerful person that you and I remember from our childhood."

"No, I have heard that."

Fiona was curious. "You know someone who has seen Grove lately?"

"He is in London now and again, I hear. I have never seen him, but I occasionally run into someone who has. He takes rooms at the Pulteney and is only here a few days."

"Oh." Grove had never written about any trips to London, but then he seldom mentioned what he did in his letters. They were polite little missives about the weather, crops, and an inquiry into Mama's health. It was entirely possible he did spend some time in London. Fiona was glad to hear it; she worried about him being out in the remote outpost of Cornwall all of the time.

The conversation slid on to other things before Lady Eliza's roving eye paused at the doorway. "Dear me, I do believe that is Lady Margaret and her niece. I daresay they were willing to come to Melbourne House because Lady Margaret is such a firm supporter of the Whigs. Otherwise, she seldom ventures out into society."

Fiona jerked around to look, her interest caught. "Lady Margaret the writer? Where?"

"Just entering the doorway. She is the stout older one wearing that dreadful rust garb. Really, one would think she would acquire a little style after all these years."

Fiona cared nothing about the lady's sartorial splendor. She was far more intrigued by the woman herself. Lady Margaret was a gifted writer whose books Fiona had read over and over again. Fiona had been both envious and delighted at the way Lady Margaret was able to bring her characters to life. If only *she* could write like that. Dare she ask this great writer to look at a small piece of her work?

"I should like to meet her," she said wistfully.

"I am sure you have heard she is reclusive and can be sharp of tongue." Lady Eliza smiled with the impishness Fiona recalled from their girlhood. "I know her slightly, and I am brave enough to introduce you."

"I should like it above all things."

Lady Eliza rose and smoothed her powder blue skirts. Fiona rose also and followed her friend across to where Lady Margaret had appropriated a chair for herself. The old woman sat grimly alone in a shadowed corner. Up close Fiona could see the tight gray curls that sat on her head like a helmet and the no-nonsense look in her eye.

Lady Eliza made the introductions. Without rising, Lady Margaret inclined her head in polite but disinterested acknowledgment.

"Fiona is a writer," Lady Eliza offered.

"Really."

Fiona stood awkwardly trying to think of something witty and clever to say. She could think of nothing.

Lady Margaret seemed to lose what little interest she had had in Fiona. Looking away, she raised her quizzing glass to observe someone across the room.

"Well, I shall leave you two to talk about writing," Lady Eliza said cheerfully. "I am persuaded you have much to discuss." She winked at Fiona and melted away.

"I so wanted to talk to you," Fiona said timidly when they were alone.

The older woman looked at her blankly. "Concerning what?"

"Writing."

"Oh, that." It was a dismissive, unencouraging statement but Fiona persevered.

"I know your book *Pastoral Piety* was a work of fiction, but I found the people so real and their plight so wrenching that I was terribly moved."

Lady Margaret inclined her head in a mannerism that was both regal and intimidating. Under ordinary circumstances, Fiona would not have tried so hard to build a conversation with someone who showed so little interest. But it was not every day that Fiona had the opportunity to talk with someone

15

of such literary stature, and she was loath to let the conversation end. "Might I sit down with you?"

Lady Margaret gestured carelessly toward the empty chair beside her.

Fiona sat. "I wanted to ask you about one of the characters I found particularly fascinating."

"Armand, of course," Lady Margaret said promptly.

"How did you know?"

"I found him fascinating myself."

"He was so—" Fiona looked around the room as she searched for the word. Suddenly her words died away. She stared across at the doorway. Standing tall and alone surveying the crowd was William Haversly.

She had known she was bound to see him some time during the Season. Constance had mentioned as much. Still, her reaction was anger at the sight of him. He was no better than the inmates of Newgate Jail. After all, he had almost killed a man. He should have remained in Spain where he had fled after shooting Grove. Instead, Lord Haversly had stayed there only a year. From all accounts his exile had been considerably sweetened by the companionship of a Spanish lady, a certain diplomat's daughter.

"You were saying," Lady Margaret prompted.

"Oh, I—I beg your pardon." Fiona tried to pick up the thread of their conversation but her thoughts were on the man who had just entered the room. Her feelings against him were all the stronger because she had once considered him a friend. He was scarcely a friend now. He had betrayed her and her family. Worse, he had destroyed Grove.

Chapter 2

FIONA CONTINUED to watch William Haversly. Beside her, Lady Margaret seemed unperturbed by the silence.

Fiona resented the self-assured way he moved about the room. Even more galling was the fact that he was received with welcoming smiles. The Melbourne House was a haven of privileged Whig aristocracy. Even those whose politics were at odds with Lord Haversly's own greeted him warmly. Fiona watched his every movement with seething resentment. How unfair that he should be so at ease and so amiably received.

She watched him talk with a group of diplomats before moving on to converse with an elderly gentleman. Then he said a few words to an aging dowager. Finally, he led the Barnett's middle daughter to the dance floor for a waltz.

Fiona was surprised at how well he performed on the dance floor. She had stood up with William often, back in the days when they were friends, and he had been only passable as a dancer. Now he executed the tight pivots of the turning steps with the ease of a master. In comparison to him, the other dancers looked like stiff marionettes.

She forced herself to look away. She refused to

admire anything about him. His presence had already ruined her evening. If she could have, she would have left. But it was Constance's first ball.

"Ah, there you are, Miss Bailey." The strong male voice at her side was a welcome diversion.

She looked up and managed a wan smile at the courtly red-haired man who bowed first to her and then to Lady Margaret.

"Good evening, Sir Giles," Fiona said.

He acknowledged her greeting with a pleasant nod before turning to the older woman. "How are you this night, Lady Margaret?"

"You need not waste your time making conversation to me, my boy," she said with asperity. "Ask the gel to dance since that is plainly why you came over here."

With an unabashed smile, Sir Giles held his hand toward Fiona. "With such encouragement, how could I not ask for the honor of standing up with you, Miss Bailey?" He winked at her.

"I should like that, Sir Giles." Still agitated by the sight of William Haversly, her words came out sounding quick and breathless.

Sir Giles escorted her onto the floor as new sets formed. The dance turned out to be an energetic reel. Constance, looking pink and flushed with pleasure, was in their set. Her bright smiles calmed Fiona. Constance was enjoying herself. That was all that mattered. Why should Fiona allow William Haversly to ruin her good time? Suddenly aware that she had missed a step, she hurried to catch up.

"It has been a long time since you were in London," Sir Giles said when the phrasing of the music brought them back together.

"Nine years."

"London has been the poorer for your absence."

She grinned at him. "Sir Giles, you were a shameless flirt nine years ago. It is reassuring to know you have not changed."

"You wound me deeply."

She laughed. "Impossible."

The easy flirtation between them helped distract her from thoughts of her enemy, although the knowledge that he was here weighed on the back of her mind.

The music ended and Sir Giles led her off the floor, bestowed a dazzling smile on her and left in search of another partner.

Fiona was standing thus alone when someone came up behind her.

"Good evening, Miss Bailey."

Even without turning she knew who the speaker was. There was no mistaking William Haversly's oaken baritone. She was tempted to walk away. She might have done so had she not noticed Lady Maxmer watching with interest. Fiona would not give that notorious gossip the satisfaction of thinking she could not deal with William Haversly.

Fiona turned slowly to face the earl. The years had been undeservingly kind to him. His carved shoulders and narrow thighs gave him the look of a sleek panther. The lean lines of what had always been a handsome face had filled out in a way that made him even more attractive. His black hair now entertained a few strands of silver. Instead of making him appear older, the gray hair made him look rakish. Although he was not a big man, he somehow managed to be imposing.

"Would you permit me to bring you a glass of ratafia?" he asked courteously.

It was the first time they had stood this close together in many years. His offer suggested he desired a truce. But he did not deserve one, and she had no intention of giving him one.

Staring directly into his dove gray eyes, she said coldly, "Not if I were dying of thirst."

A bored smile settled over his face. "You must call me should that event ever occur. You might then decide that you would like some refreshment after all."

"Lord Haversly, I do not find you amusing. I only speak to you at all because we are in polite society. Pray do not presume we are to pretend to like each other or that you can expect me to extend more than the most basic civilities. You are a common criminal who just happens to have enough money and position to convince society to forget your crime. But I shall never forget what you did." Aflame, she no longer cared who was watching her or what they thought of her actions.

"Grove was not blameless in that affair," he said tightly. The gray eyes bore into her. "Has it ever occurred to you that you have only heard his side of the story?"

"Indeed," she said coldly. "I do not doubt you could tell quite a credible tale now. After all, you have had all these years to invent one. Even as a boy you could be most convincing in your lies." Contempt underscored her every word. "Your actions at the time, however, spoke loudly. If you were innocent, then why did you flee the country?"

"It was a mistake," he said quietly. "I should have stayed."

She had heard of people who eventually convinced themselves of their own lies. She did not know if the earl believed himself or if he merely hoped she would. "I have nothing more to say to you." Whirling, Fiona walked away. Let Lady Maxmer's tongue wag; she did not care. She could stand only so much conversation with William Haversly.

Marching up to the refreshment table with her rose skirts swirling, she requested a cup of punch. As the waiter handed it to her, she was surprised to discover that her hands were trembling.

Lady Eliza came up beside her. She opened and closed her fan in a careless gesture, but she watched Fiona closely. "My dear, you know that I would not interfere in your affairs for the world."

"Then why do I have the strongest of suspicions that you are about to?" Fiona asked darkly. She was not in a mood to be charitable with anyone.

"It is only that you must have a care how you treat Lord Haversly. Pray do not look at me as if you wish to run me through. I am not saying you must *like* him, only that you must be careful not to let your feelings show too strongly in public. You came to London for Constance's presentation. Nothing must mar that. If it becomes too obvious there are old wounds festering between your family and Lord Haversly's, certain eligible men might shy away from your sister. For appearance's sake, you must present a good front."

"How could 'old wounds' not fester?" Fiona demanded. "He behaved without any honor or dignity."

"That's as may be," Eliza said reasonably. "You must remember that there is little love lost between some very powerful families in London, but they put up a good front when it is necessary. They have even been known to entertain each other."

"Are you suggesting I should pretend Lord Haversly and I are friends?"

"Of course not. But to be openly hostile with him will not serve you well. You must remember that some people know nothing about the duel. Those who do may think all has been resolved in the years since it happened. Lord Haversly has become a powerful force in Parliament and has undertaken a worthy cause in his campaign to help the factory children. Many people have great respect for him. Even those who disagree with him acknowledge he is a persuasive orator. He spends all year in London in Parliament and on many committees. He is known and received everywhere. You would do well to remember that."

"I would not wish Constance to marry anyone who respected Lord Haversly," Fiona retorted.

"That is your anger, not your sense, speaking. Think about what I have said."

After a moment of bitter reflection, Fiona was forced to admit that Eliza was right. Constance's chance to make a perfect match should not be jeopardized by anything.

"You see that I am correct," Eliza said.

"Yes, and I dislike you for it."

"Of course you do, my dear." Her companion patted her cheek and floated away.

Fiona drank her punch and called for a second cup. The punch was only lightly spiced with alcohol. One more drink could not possibly hurt. She had a third one. Perhaps she had a fourth; she could not recall.

All she knew was the drink blurred her thoughts and dulled the flint edge of her anger. She even relaxed enough to chat with some old friends and to dance, although with less grace than usual. At least she was able to push aside thoughts of Lord Haversly, although she occasionally did look at him. It was difficult to be in a room with him and forget his presence. She despised him, but now and again she could not help thinking of earlier days when they had laughed together and had been friends.

She had another cup of punch.

Fiona was humming tunelessly by the time she was handed into the carriage for the drive home. Mrs. Dyer looked at her with surprise, then her mouth turned downward in disapproval.

Constance giggled at her.

"The carriage is jolting frightfully," Fiona complained. "I am having a difficult time sitting upright."

"We have not yet started," Mrs. Dyer said tersely before folding her hands and turning to look out the window.

"Oh." Fiona turned to her sister. "Did you have a good time?"

"It was splendid! I do believe several gentlemen will call on me tomorrow. They asked permission of Mrs. Dyer to do so."

Mrs. Dyer nodded. "Indeed they did. Very proper young men they all were, too."

"Good." Fiona settled back against the soft squabs. She was pleased at the attention Constance had received tonight. Still, something nagging at the back of her mind prevented her from being as satisfied as she should have been. Eventually, the gentle rocking of the carriage worked its magic, and she fell asleep without ever discovering why she felt unsettled.

"I know our families have been at odds for years, but you have never really told me what happened."

William watched from behind his cluttered, over-sized desk as his younger brother moved about the study. James always seemed filled with restless energy, but today more so than usual. He picked up a mottled book, leafed through the pages without looking at them, then laid it on a walnut side table. He set the globe in the corner spinning before moving aimlessly over to the diamond-shaped windowpanes and drumming his fingers against them.

William sighed and looked at the stack of work on his desk. There were letters of petition from factory workers, bits of facts from various ministries, and notes he had jotted to himself during committee meetings. "James, I am very busy. Can we not talk another time? I am making a speech in Parliament tomorrow, and I still have much writing to do." It was an important speech on the rights of children not to have to work fourteen- and fifteen-hour days.

Ignoring him, James cleared off a space and perched on the edge of the desk. "Well, *did* you shoot Grove Bailey?"

"Yes."

"Why?"

"We were fighting a duel," William said crustily. "I believe it is customary to shoot at the other party under those circumstances. He was most assuredly aiming at me."

"What was the duel about?"

William irritably pushed back his chair and rose. "Devil take it, James. We were both nineteen. We were impetuous and full of ourselves and much too ready to take offense. Before I knew what was happening, he was talking about seconds and meeting at Putney Heath at dawn."

In the silence that followed, William wondered

why he did not simply tell his brother the whole truth. But then he would have to tell the role he had played and offer explanations. It would have been a lot easier to explain what had happened if he had not left for the Continent immediately after the duel. But he had been young and foolish and had thought it necessary. Now he saw that that action had only painted him with a blacker brush. He tried for an abbreviated explanation. "Grove and I fought because he led me into a dishonorable situation."

James gazed silently at William as if waiting for him to say more.

William sighed but was about to launch into a more complete explanation when James slid off the edge of the desk and announced, "I am going to White's."

"Fine." His brother's attention never stayed fixed on one subject long, and William was not surprised that it had wandered from this one. William wondered what had prompted the whole discussion in the first place. As a rule, the young cawker had nothing more on his mind than making the short, fashionable walk from Watier's to White's to change his game from macao to whist. It was just as well this particular subject had been left alone. It was not one William enjoyed talking about, he reflected as he sat back down, put on his glasses, and began to read.

In a time of great politicians, William was flattered that his name was beginning to be mentioned as one of them. It was said he was becoming as important as the versatile and brilliant Brougham. William knew he had not yet achieved the debating skills of Peel, but he was pleased that some counted his mastery of facts equal to Huskisson's. Certainly more than one person had mentioned the resonance of his voice when he spoke.

But he had not become a politician because he wanted to stand up in the House of Commons and hear himself speak. He had become involved because he wanted to help those less fortunate. William admired Wilberforce, who had used his eloquence and conviction toward emancipating blacks. The most important battle now was to improve the lot of factory children. William aligned himself strongly with Lord Ashley in the fight.

William had five people on his personal payroll out gathering facts from the factories of northern England. He hoped they would soon have something to report to refute the testimony that was being given before the committee by physicians and overseers who insisted the factory children were well attended to. William did not believe a word of it. So many of them would not die or become permanent cripples if the work were light and nondemanding.

Even though he cared greatly for the cause, he was unable to concentrate on it at the moment. He continued to read, but the words ran together on the page until they made no sense. He found himself rereading the same paragraph a third time.

Sighing, he leaned back in the chair and gazed up at the elaborate fretwork on the ceiling.

His conversation with Fiona Bailey at Melbourne House had disturbed him.

Last night was the first time he had stood close to her in nine years. The blue eyes that had once been so frank and open were now clouded with suspicion. At times, however, he thought he had glimpsed past her cool wall of distrust to the vulnerable girl she had once been.

What a carefree, sparkling chit she had been at fifteen. He remembered how her laughter had hung in the air as she raced her pony against him across the meadow. He could still see her radiant, innocent smile as it had looked those last, lingering summers of her childhood. Watching her become a woman had been a revelation, especially to a boy who was himself becoming a man.

Her figure had changed ever so subtly. Her laughter had become more husky. Her coltish movements became the movements of the willow when a gentle breeze catches it—graceful, evocative. All of the men in the neighborhood began to look at her in a different way. Masculine boots that had once been polished only at the insistence of mothers were now carefully inspected. The matter of what jacket to wear gained in importance.

William's family had been friends with Fiona's family. A match between himself and Fiona would certainly have been well received. There had been times when their gazes had seemed to meet and hold in a special way.

Then she went to London for a Season.

Then he shot her brother.

William jerked himself upright and forced himself to return to working on his speech. Any rapport or friendship he had shared with a younger Fiona and with Grove was all ashes now and had been for years. He had far more important things to do than lament its passing.

Chapter 3

"ARE WE ready to leave?" Constance demanded.

Fiona nodded reluctantly and put down a book. The two sisters were at Thisle's Mayfair lending library. Fiona would have been content to spend the whole day there. She wished she could pull each book out and look at it. She wanted to run her fingers down the spines of the books, and she wanted to smell the leather and bindery paste.

Beside her, however, Constance looked as if she would go wild if they spent another moment in the small, tastefully decorated lending library. It was not like Hookum's or Colburn's circulating libraries that carried such drivel as Minerva Novels or titles like *The Miraculous Nuptials*. This library carried only true literature.

"Fiona, ple-ase . . ."

Repressing her disappointment, Fiona picked up the books she had selected and the two sisters left.

"I cannot see how you can devote so much time to looking at books," Constance complained as she trotted down the marble steps toward the carriage.

Fiona was wounded. "I am a writer." At her sister's sidelong glance, she acknowledged, "It is true I have never published anything, but I hope to someday." She hugged the books in her arms defensively.

"I find inspiration in what good writers have written. Sometimes I get ideas from them."

Constance stifled a yawn.

"You may not find my work important but others are not so disinterested." Fiona was still excited about the invitation to Lady Margaret's house that had arrived this morning. As she settled inside the carriage, she recalled the invitation verbatim. *Dear Miss Bailey, I am entertaining a few friends who amuse themselves by writing. We sometimes gather to discuss our works-in-progress and to offer each other gentle criticisms. I hope you will honor us with your presence Thursday next in the afternoon. We meet just after teatime. Yours, etc., Lady Margaret*

"Could we stop at the milliners?" Constance asked. "I have no hat presentable enough to wear about in public."

Fiona looked at her askance. "What utter nonsense. You have a dozen lovely bonnets. We have been buying them these six weeks past."

"They all make me look like a schoolgirl." Constance's pout was not unlike a schoolgirl's. "I want something that will make me look sophisticated. We might also stop at Mr. Botibol's and look at his ostrich and fancy feathers to put on some of my other hats. They are all so dreadful. I have nothing fetching to wear."

"Fetching," Fiona repeated with interest. "Dear me, it sounds to me as if you have found a young man you wish to impress."

Constance colored.

"Who is he?"

"We were talking about hats, not men."

"Of course," Fiona stifled a smile. She would not press if her sister did not wish to talk about an infatuation. It was early in the Season, and Constance had all the time in the world to have half a dozen more tendres before she settled on a man to marry. Meanwhile, Fiona was relieved that her sister's unsuitable attachment for James Haversly was over. "If you wish to stop at the milliner's, certainly we shall. While we are out, I must stop at the stationer's. I have not written to Mama in three days."

"Nor I," Constance confessed. "Give her my love when you write."

Their mother had been in fragile health for the past few years and had not been well enough to travel to London. Fiona had hated going away and leaving Mama alone, but she knew she was in capable hands among servants who had been with the family for years. Still, Fiona tried to write home often and to tell her all about the routs and parties they were attending. Mama enjoyed hearing the little details of their day. Of course she was most interested in Constance's social progress, and she wrote back especially enthusiastic letters whenever Fiona reported what parties and dinners they had been invited to.

The next day when Fiona did write to her mother, she told about her invitation to Lady Margaret's. She also described the hat Constance had searched for so diligently. The two sisters went into half a dozen shops before Constance found what she wanted—a large, black velvet hat with a sculpted brim. It had not looked magnificent on the shelf, but when Constance put it on and tilted it just so, it became positively alluring. Constance had looked beguiling and worldly.

The hat made Fiona uncomfortable. "Would you

not like something a little more youthful?" she had suggested hopefully.

No, the black one was exactly the hat Constance wanted, and they had left the shop with it swinging from Constance's hand in a pretty flowered box.

Fiona finished her letter, blew on it to dry the ink, then folded it carefully.

"Are you ready?" Constance called up the stairs.

Fiona looked toward the ormolu clock on the mantel of her small writing room. Was it already time to go riding? Goodness, it was.

She hurried out into the hall and leaned over the banister. "I shall be down in a moment. She started to turn, then paused. Constance looked exquisite in a jade-colored cloak with black trim and the black hat sitting sleekly over her blond curls.

Fiona had intended to wear her own rust-colored riding habit. Considering what Constance was wearing, however, it seemed dreadfully démodé. Instead, she had Dorothea help her into her new peacock-green riding habit. As she descended the stairs, Constance frowned up at her.

"Are you trying to overshadow me, Fiona?"

"I hardly think that possible." Still, when Fiona caught a glimpse of herself striding by the cheval glass, she was pleased. A healthy glow showed on her cheeks, and her eyes looked deep and blue against the peacock green of her outfit.

The day was cool and crisp, and dark clouds suggested rain. But they were dressed, and they went to the park anyway. There Fiona saw that the weather had not deterred the hundreds of fashionable riders who jammed Rotten Row vying to see and be seen. Fiona rode on the outside and Constance in the center. From her position, Fiona could still smile and nod to acquaintances and take the measure of the young men who cast glances toward Constance.

There were many who did.

Fiona sized each of them up. Viscount Mersey would be an exceptional choice, Fiona thought as he tipped his hat. Constance, however, barely glanced at him. Ah, well. Lord Henderson also looked in their direction and slowed his mount so that it would take him longer to pass. He would surely be acceptable, Fiona thought, since he was handsome and very well to pass. Flirtation was in his eyes, but Constance smiled blandly at him and made no attempt to slow her horse. Fiona looked regretfully over her shoulder. Such a nice smile. If she were a bit younger herself . . .

When she swung forward in the saddle, she found herself looking directly at Lord Haversly. Her instinct was to turn away. But she reminded herself what Lady Eliza had said. It would not do to give him the cut direct, especially not when the park was crowded with the ton. Biting her lip, she nodded vaguely toward him.

He seemed surprised by the gesture of recognition. He pulled his mount to a halt beside them. "Good afternoon, ladies."

Constance smiled prettily at him.

Fiona fought down the temptation to spur her horse forward.

The earl's gray-eyed gaze went to Constance.

There was little Fiona could do but introduce them formally. "Lord Haversly, allow me to present my sister, Miss Bailey." Of course he had known Constance when she was a child, but the rift had occurred when she was only eight. It galled Fiona to be obliged to introduce them now.

Her sister smiled with greater force than was necessary. "It is so nice to make your acquaintance, milord. One hears such wonderful things about the work you are doing in Parliament."

Fiona cast a sideways glance at her sister. Since when had Constance paid the least attention to politics?

His voice was deep and smooth, laced with that baritone inflection that echoed so familiarly from the past. "I am flattered that you would notice, Miss Bailey. A young lady enjoying her first Season is often preoccupied with other things."

His smile seemed more polished and less sincere than Fiona remembered. Of course, it had never really *been* sincere, she reminded herself. She had only been young and foolish enough to think it was. She had been equally duped by the intensity of that gaze. In the past when they had talked, she had felt herself being pulled toward him by the force of his gaze, leaning toward him as if something exciting were about to occur.

". . . while I am not entirely versed in politics, I do admire those who are," Constance was saying. "You must be very busy all the time."

"I am often occupied."

"That probably accounts for why you are at so few parties. You are missing a wonderful time."

He smiled kindly. "The parties are not so exciting at my advanced age."

"Fiona is near your age, and she loves them," Constance objected.

William transferred his gaze to her. "Do you?" he asked, the gray eyes rich with interest.

"They can be amusing." They had lingered long enough, Fiona decided. Restless horses were beginning to back up behind them. Fiona interrupted, "It was good to speak with you, Lord Haversly. You must excuse us, however."

He bowed courteously.

Fiona urged her horse forward and her sister followed.

"Thank you for introducing me," Constance said when she caught up. "I feared you would ignore him. You always have in Surrey."

"I would dearly love to ignore the man," Fiona muttered. "But it has been brought to my attention that doing so might create problems for you. He has become quite important and is received everywhere."

"They say he works very hard in Parliament."

Fiona guided her horse around a tree and the pair fell into silence as they continued down Rotten Row.

Not ten minutes later, Constance turned to her. "Are you ready to leave? I am tired."

Fiona was startled. Tired? Since when did a girl of Constance's age grow weary from a tame ride through the park? It seemed more likely she had accomplished whatever she had intended when she donned the black hat and fetching riding habit. Fiona was confused. The purpose of those feminine snares must have been to attract the notice of a man. Yet Constance had shown no interest in any of the men they had passed. Perhaps whomever she had hoped to see had not come. Yet she seemed in good spirits and showed no disappointment.

Ah, well, if Constance wished to leave, then Fiona was not going to make too much of it. It would be good to get back in time to work on her book. Constance could rest before the round of "at homes" tonight.

* * *

Four days after the ride in the park, Fiona sat with Mrs. Dyer in the pink parlor that overlooked a garden abloom with honeysuckle. The sweet scent crept in through the open window and battled for dominance over the scent of roses and lilies of the valley that covered the room.

The flowers had been gifts from callers. The parlor was vacant of company for the first time in several hours. All morning a steady stream of men had called on Constance. Fiona had been pleased at how many had come and had greeted each with an encouraging smile. Constance, on the other hand, had been pleasant but vague. At the root of her smile, Fiona suspected disinterest.

"She is wise not to encourage any particular suitor," Mrs. Dyer said placidly. Her needle slipped in and out of the pillowcase she was busy embroidering.

Fiona was not convinced. Over the past week, her sister had been the center of attention at every ball and fete. When they went to the theater two nights ago, men crowded around their box so thickly at the intermissions that they could hardly breathe. When Fiona and Constance attended a military review yesterday, they scarcely saw the soldiers marching for the tide of suitors. Notes and poems arrived on a daily basis.

The parlor had become a hothouse of flowers sent by yearning gentlemen. Fiona was pleased beyond all measure by the showing of attention. Some of society's finest were clearly smitten by Constance. It only remained for her sister to return the interest.

There was the rub. Constance remained aloof and detached. Fiona could not help recalling the episode at St. Paul's with a sense of unease. For whose benefit had she purchased the black hat? Was she harboring a tendre for someone totally unsuitable? That would explain why she seemed so disinclined to encourage any of the eligible men vying for her attention. Surely, Fiona hoped, Constance was not clinging to an interest in James Haversly.

She laid aside the pages she had been trying to proofread and rose. Driven by nervous energy, she crossed the room to arrange a bouquet of white roses in their crystal vase. As if the matter of Constance was not worrisome enough, Fiona had other things on her mind.

The servants who had come with her for the Season had been accustomed to the calm pace of Surrey. Not all were adjusting well to London. Specifically, the coachman Mr. Sanders was showing an alarming tendency to patronize a nearby ale establishment. Two times last week it had been necessary for him to be carried home from the alehouse.

Fiona had spoken with Mr. Sanders this morning, but that did not mean the problem was solved. Sighing, she reflected how difficult it was for a woman to manage a household alone. A man could have been more blunt, and his word would have carried more weight. Although the coachman had listened with head bowed, hat in hand, she was not certain he was cured. Or even sincerely penitent.

In addition to that concern, something else was at the root of her nervousness. Today was Thursday—the day she was to meet with Lady Margaret and her circle of writers.

Setting aside the vase of roses, Fiona returned to the papers she had laid on the chair. She read the first sentence again, and panic crept over her. This was terrible. How could she have told Lady Margaret she was a writer? She was a fraud. This was no more writing than a child's scratches. She did not have the nerve to present anything this afternoon for the consideration and criticism of *real* writers.

"I must send a message to Lady Margaret," she announced to Mrs. Dyer in sudden agitation. "I have to tell her I shall be unable to attend this afternoon."

The chaperone looked up. "I thought you had been looking forward to going. You have certainly spoken of it often these past few days."

"No," Fiona said quickly. "I do not wish to go. I—I am too busy. I shall send a note 'round telling her I cannot come."

Mrs. Dyer shrugged and turned back to her embroidery. "Surely there is no need to do that."

Fiona stared bleakly at the papers dangling from her fingers and confessed, "I do not know if it is any good."

"I am certain it is fine." Mrs. Dyer broke a length of red thread with a sharp snap of her teeth and proceeded to thread a needle with blue thread.

Fiona was silent. People who did not write could not understand the agony that went into every page, every sentence. To then offer this precious effort for criticism was frightening.

The clock struck.

"It is almost teatime," she murmured aloud.

"They are expecting you and may be disappointed if you do not come."

Fiona fidgeted with a cameo pin on her shoulder. If she did not attend, she might never be invited to join the group again. Some of her resolve began to return. This was no time to be a coward. If she was ever to know her worth as a writer, she must present her work for appraisal.

"You are right, Mrs. Dyer; I should go to Lady Margaret's."

"I am certain you will enjoy it."

Perhaps not enjoy it, but Fiona thought she would benefit from it. Rising, she went upstairs and looked in her closet for something suitable to wear to the meeting. Finally she selected a royal blue gown with a high bodice. The broad frilled collar looked expensive—it was—and the little half boots were respectable.

Dorothea helped her dress. As if she sensed Fiona's apprehension, she said little, but her hands were soothing as she worked the buttons and brushed Fiona's hair into a style of simple elegance.

When Fiona was ready, she looked herself full in the mirror. "You are a superb writer," she told her reflection but did not believe a word of it.

Fighting down nervousness, she set off for the meeting.

Across town quite a different meeting was taking place in William's book-lined study.

James stared defiantly at his older brother. "I wish to call on her, William. Why should I not? She is being presented this Season. The purpose of presenting chits is for them to find suitable marriage partners. I am not some cinder sifter, you know. I am a perfectly acceptable choice."

"Miss Constance Bailey's sister hates our family— a little detail you seem to keep forgetting."

James threw himself off the sofa. "Dash it all, I am young, handsome—"

"Modest," William interjected dryly.

"I have eight thousand pounds a year. When I turn five-and-twenty that will be double. It is scarcely something for a woman to turn down lightly. She has a fortune, of course, but our family is of greater social standing than hers," he added, and made an irritable swipe at his hair. William supposed the gesture was meant to brush it down but had quite the opposite effect. "Their father was only a baronet. If you were to die, I could be an earl."

"You cheer me no end with your happy thoughts, James."

The younger man made another tight turn. "Dash it all, I want to see her."

William looked at his brother with heightened curiosity. He had thought James's interest in Constance Bailey would pass quickly. Most things did with James. Instead, this seemed to be deepening. "Just how serious are you about her?"

James flushed and looked away. "I enjoy her company. She is devilish pretty."

"I know." William remembered well how Fiona had bubbled with the same sparkle young Constance had. Having grown up with Fiona, it had come as a shock to William the first time he had seen Fiona in a low-cut gown. He remembered how embarrassed she had been by the display of bosom. He, on the other hand, had been thunderstruck. And intrigued. William almost regretted that James had missed that sense of awe at seeing Constance turn from a child into a woman. Then he reminded himself of the obstacles between the families and realized James's interest could not come to anything anyway.

The younger man paced the room with long, impatient steps. "What is to prevent me from presenting my card at the door like any normal person? For pity's sake, that jackal Henderson is calling on her. Henderson," he repeated contemptuously. "He spends half his time at the Israelitish establishment borrowing money."

William tipped his chair back and examined the ceiling. "Is it possible you are only so intent on this girl because she is unattainable?"

"Do not be insulting. We have been watching each other in church over the past several months in Surrey."

"Oh? How spiritual." William drawled.

"You may make sport of it, but it was the only means we had of seeing each other. We took what we could get."

"I would have thought you more resourceful than that, James."

A small smile crossed his brother's face. "I did manage to meet her in the forest a time or two. We gave her maid a few guineas to look away for a few moments."

William straightened abruptly, all traces of amusement gone. "You bribed her maid to leave you two alone? You had trysts in the woods with an un-chaperoned girl?"

"Do not make it sound sordid, William. You have my word it was very chaste. Well, I did steal a kiss or two," he admitted.

"I nothing doubt you did," William said tersely. This had gone further than he had suspected. "Well, you will have to forget her. If the girl's father were alive he would not countenance your courting his daughter. Fiona will not allow it either."

"The disagreeable shrew," James said bitterly.

"You will please refrain from calling ladies by such terms, whatever your opinion of them,"

William said with a sharpness that surprised even himself.

"Why must I be polite? You have never made any secret of the fact you dislike her."

"That has nothing to say to the matter. We are in London now, and we must behave like civilized people."

"Civilized people call on each other."

William sighed. "Do not be tiresome, James. There are plenty of other chits available. Form an attachment to one of them."

On hearing that note of brotherly wisdom, James stomped out.

William watched him go, then tried to turn his attention back to his work. He had far too much to do to pass his afternoons arguing with James. Certainly it was pointless to try to change the past. If the truth were known, it was he who should forbid his brother to have any intercourse with the Baileys. It was ironic that Fiona thought James beyond the pale when the facts were very much otherwise.

Chapter 4

FIONA HAD no sooner arrived home from Lady Margaret's than Constance caught her. "Where have you been? Did you not remember we are to go to Vauxhall Gardens this evening?"

Fiona stood at the bottom of the staircase, her hand arrested in the act of unfastening the frogs on her pelisse. She stared at her sister. "You did not say anything about wanting to go to the gardens tonight."

"Yes, I did. I mentioned it yesterday; you simply were not attending."

"But I have just returned from Lady Margaret's," Fiona objected. "I had no plans to go out this evening." In fact, she had looked forward to spending the evening studying the notes and critiques that had been given her concerning the chapter she had taken to the writers' group.

"Mrs. Dyer and I could go alone," Constance said.

"No, I will go with you." Fiona did not like the idea of Constance at the gardens with only Mrs. Dyer. While the chaperone was suitable enough, the place was questionable. The paths were not only bounded with high hedges, they were poorly lit. It was easy to get lost in the maze, and scoundrels had been known to lurk in the shadows and steal kisses from startled maidens. Since the gardens were open to the public, a mixture of ruffians and the ton frequented it. That made it both exciting and dangerous.

"Very well. I wish to leave by nine, please." Having delivered that announcement, Constance lifted her apricot skirts and proceeded up the stairs.

Fiona bit her lip, disappointed that she had been deprived of the opportunity to relax and reflect on this afternoon. The meeting had been frightening and exhilarating. Lady Margaret had told her she had potential. The old writer had gone on to say there were problems with motive and characterization and plotting in Fiona's story. But she *had* said, "You have potential." As Fiona started up the steps, she rolled those words over and over in her mind.

Four other writers had been present. One was a lady who wrote poetry. The three men were all published writers of fiction. Fiona had been awed. They had not brimmed with wild acclaim for her work, but they had said she had a talent that could be developed.

Upstairs in her room, she found Dorothea folding linens.

"I must get ready for this evening. We are going to Vauxhall Gardens."

The maid put aside the linens. "What do you wish to wear?"

"The Devonshire brown dress edged with cord." It was plain but a sensible choice for an evening in the chilly London air. Fiona only hoped Constance did not wish to stay too late at the gardens. While she could see that they would hold a fascination for a young girl, they made her uneasy.

Twenty minutes later Dorothea stood back from fastening the dress and reached for a brush.

"There's no need to fuss with my hair. I shall be wearing a bonnet."

"As you wish."

Fiona left the room and headed down the stairs. From the landing she saw Constance's silver-threaded shawl fluttering as her sister paced restlessly. It was a very stylish shawl to wear to Vauxhall Gardens, Fiona thought fleetingly.

Constance spied her and started for the door. "Hurry. I cannot imagine what took you so long."

Fiona quickened her pace. In the hallway, Mrs. Dyer fell into step behind the sisters and followed them out the door.

"Why such haste, Constance? The gardens are open until very late."

"Yes, but I am most anxious to see them; I have heard so much about them." She sat in the carriage and smoothed down the fringes of her shawl.

It seemed a long and jolting ride before they reached the gardens. For the price of a shilling, they entered walks dotted with triumphal arches. Through the arches, Fiona peered at paintings of the ruins of Palmyra. They were appropriately gaudy.

"Aren't they splendid?" Constance demanded.

"Quite," Fiona murmured.

"Everything looks wonderful. I want to see the whole of the grounds."

Mrs. Dyer tightened her black wool coat around her shoulders with a look of resignation.

"And we must have one of the suppers. They are said to have the most delicious pastries."

As they proceeded to tour the grounds, the festive air, the dancing lanterns, and the colorful mix of people began to catch Fiona up in the sense of excitement.

There was something innocently amusing about the "musical bushes," even though one knew that musicians sat just beyond the shrubbery in a hollowed-out place in the ground and did the playing. And the large wooden rotunda where they stopped to listen to the orchestra was as much a place to be seen as Rotten Row at the fashionable hour. Above all, it was fun for Fiona to be with Constance when she was looking at everything with sparkling, alert eyes.

They sat in one of the supper boxes tucked away next to the grove and ate. The boxes were painted with scenes of a maypole dance, and Constance looked entranced with the little scene as she traced it with her finger. Fiona ate her ice cream and cherries and smiled. Even Mrs. Dyer seemed to unbend after sampling a few of the fresh fruits.

After supper, they again mingled and saw a number of people they knew. Constance stopped to chat with a friend and then with a pair of dandies. Not long afterward, Fiona spied Lady Eliza on the arm of her tall, balding husband Arthur.

"Eliza, you simply must come to tea so that we can have a nice coze." She had twice sent invitations, but Eliza had not responded.

"I shall sometime," her friend said.

Was it the uneven light from the lanterns that made Eliza's face look so pale? No, those really were dark half-moons under her eyes. It occurred to Fiona she had not seen Eliza at the last two parties she had attended.

"I hope you are well." She put a warm hand on Eliza's cool one.

Eliza's husband put his arm protectively around his wife's shoulders. "She is only a bit tired tonight."

"Of course." Fiona was not convinced.

Arthur took over the conversation. "I understand your brother now lives in Cornwall near St. Agnes."

"Yes." Fiona supposed he meant to be friendly, but it sounded more like an accusation.

"I have business that occasionally takes me there, and I have friends there. They say they do not see much of him."

"He is a retiring person," she murmured. "He—"

Fiona was interrupted by Constance tugging on her arm. "Look up at the sky! Fireworks."

She looked upward just as patches of brilliant white burst across the dark sky.

The younger woman was enchanted. "How delightful! Could we move out of the shadow of the trees so that we might see better? Over by that fountain, perhaps."

"Of course, dear." Fiona exchanged a few words of parting with her friends, then followed Mrs. Dyer and her impatient sister.

There were already a number of people standing around the fountain when they reached it.

"I believe it would be easier to see from the other side," Constance said.

"I think it is all of a piece, and one can see as well from here," Mrs. Dyer remarked.

Fiona was inclined to agree but made no argument as Constance threaded her way to the other side. Fiona was following when her sister stopped so abruptly Fiona almost walked into her.

"Why, good evening, Mr. Haversly," Constance said in a breathy little voice.

Fiona came to a dead halt and stared at the man whose face was sharply illuminated by a burst of fireworks. James Haversly.

46

Constance turned to a second man and curtsied. "Lord Haversly. How nice to see you."

Fiona turned to see William Haversly standing straight and proper beside his brother. For a shilling she would have wrung Constance's neck. Mrs. Dyer nodded to each of the gentlemen and then faded into the background, pretending an interest in the fireworks. Naturally she knew of the long-standing animosity between the families, and Fiona was certain she was listening to see what transpired now that the four of them had been brought together.

"Good evening, Lord Haversly, Mr. Haversly," Fiona said to each in turn. Her crisp brevity and lack of a smile did not prevent Constance from chattering excitedly to the two men.

"What a surprise to see you here! Of course, so many people come to the gardens that it is not really surprising to see you here. Is it not a very pleasant evening? I am so glad we came." Constance's shawl fluttered with her gestures, its silver threads catching in the light and shimmering. James's eyes never left her sister's face, Fiona noted.

"Have you gentlemen been here long?" Fiona forced herself to ask, mindful of Mrs. Dyer's presence and that she must make some show of politeness.

"Not long," Lord Haversly answered.

Had they been here long *waiting,* Fiona should have said. She had no doubt this meeting had been arranged earlier. What took her aback was that Lord Haversly should have been involved in the planning.

"It is getting cooler," Constance observed to no one in particular.

"It is not *too* cool for you, is it, Miss Bailey?" James asked in a worried voice. "I could send someone for a heavier wrap if you are cold."

"No, I am fine."

"Are you certain?"

Fiona pursed her lips. He need not act as if Constance were a fragile flower who would perish with the night air. As for her sister, it was not necessary for her to stand so near James Haversly and encourage his conversation and attention.

The fireworks continued in the night sky above them, but Fiona had no interest. The two younger people gazed raptly at the sky together. Lord Haversly lingered somewhere off to the side. She purposely did not look at him, even though she sensed he was watching her. It might have been his presence even more than the fact her sister was standing beside James Haversly that provoked Fiona to act.

"It is time we were leaving, Constance."

"So soon?"

"Yes."

Constance, even in her befuddled state, must have heard the firmness in Fiona's voice. Reluctantly, she turned to say good-bye to their male companions.

"It is time we left as well," James said. "Besides, I should not like for three ladies to walk alone in such a place as this."

"We shall be perfectly fine," Fiona said. Was it her imagination, or did he look at her with dislike? Not that it mattered what his feelings were, but since *his* brother had shot her brother, James Haversly had no reason to find her objectionable.

"I insist," he said.

She would have refused even more strongly had she not noticed an unsavory-looking man watching the interchange. Uneasy thoughts of the man following them down a dark path decided her. "Very well," she said briskly.

James fell into step beside Constance. Mrs. Dyer aligned herself beside her young charge. That left no room on the walk for Fiona. She followed the threesome. William fell in beside her, his heavy boots crunching on the loose gravel.

She recalled the encounter in Hyde Park and wondered if her sister's objective in going there had been to meet the earl and somehow enlist him in her cause. Fiona glanced toward her companion as they passed beneath a lamp.

He was well turned out in a buff jacket and black breeches. His cravat was tied in a knot made all the more effective for its simplicity. She disliked him the more because there was so little about his outward appearance with which to find fault.

He glanced at her.

"Did you have a hand in arranging tonight's meeting?" she asked frankly.

His laugh was low and mirthless. "If you think I wish to promote a romance between my brother and your sister, you are fair and far-out. I came here out of boredom and chanced upon my brother once I arrived. He seemed as unhappy at seeing me here as you appeared to be to see him. And me," he added with a significant look in her direction.

"You can scarcely be surprised if I am not elated at the sight of you," Fiona said tartly.

This time his chuckle held some humor. "No, Fiona, I do not expect elation when you see me. It is an interesting concept to ponder, though," he added thoughtfully, "the picture of you smiling and greeting me agreeably."

She ignored that.

"I saw Lady Eliza earlier," he said.

"I saw her, too."

"I am afraid she is not well."

"I do not think so either," she agreed.

Both were silent. Fiona wondered if he was thinking back to the times she and Eliza had acted like young hoydens while he and Grove had looked on and laughed. Eliza had been young and vibrant then. They all had. They had believed themselves to be invincible then.

"They are going to Bath so that she may take the waters. Perhaps that will cure whatever is wrong with her."

"I hope so," she said.

They walked in silence for several more minutes. Ahead of them Fiona saw Constance's head bobbing in animation. Her laughter floated backward like music from a seductive oboe. James bent low to hear her words.

The little parade moved away from the crowd and into the unlit paths. Fiona remained keenly aware of the man beside her. He seemed to loom larger in the darkness. She could not imagine any rogue tangling with the earl.

Minutes passed and still they followed the dark path. She frowned. There must be a faster way back to their carriage. If there was, however, those in the lead did not take it.

Fiona was startled out of her thoughts by a firm masculine hand on her elbow. Lord Haversly led her around a puddle, then wordlessly let go of her.

"I—Thank you." His touch unsettled her.

The silence between them grew uncomfortable. Of course there was nothing at all for them to say, but she could not help thinking back to younger days when conversation between them had tumbled so effortlessly forward. It suddenly seemed impossible to remain beside him any longer.

Fiona hurried ahead and caught up with Constance. "Is there not a faster way to the carriage? I think the last path would have led us directly to it."

"A faster way?" Constance repeated dreamily.

"I am persuaded we are taking the quickest course," James said.

Fiona whirled toward him. "You do not even know where our carriage is, Mr. Haversly."

"That is true, but this would seem, overall, to be a faster route to, um, to most things."

She stared at him. The man—on top of being a Haversly—was an idiot. How could her sister have any interest in him? It was clear he was nothing more than a handsome suit of clothes. Yes, she conceded, he was also possessed of a well-proportioned body and a smile that some women might find charming. He had, in short, all the physical attributes of his older brother. But he was not worthy of Constance.

"I wish to reach the carriage as quickly as possible," Fiona stated.

Five minutes later they stood beside it. James handed Constance inside with much courtliness and many lingering looks. Mrs. Dyer climbed in behind her.

Fiona turned to the men. "Thank you for your escort. I hope you have a good evening." Then she got into the carriage and waited for the door to close. Her thoughts were clouded with the tension and anxiousness she felt from being with Lord Haversly. His speculation about what it would be like if she expressed joy at seeing him had been impertinent. She would be glad when the Season ended and she no longer had to see him at all.

Fiona had no doubt Constance had arranged to meet James Haversly at the fountain. And she was furious about it. She intended to ring a peal over her sister's head as soon as they were alone. She valiantly held her tongue throughout the carriage ride home since it would not do to create a scene in front of Mrs. Dyer.

As she sat in the dark carriage, Fiona was also distracted by jumbled thoughts about Lord Haversly. Seeing him again after all these years stirred up memories. She recalled a fair that she and Grove had attended with William when she was nine. She remembered exactly where she had dropped a stitch in the handkerchief she had embroidered for William when she was twelve. She remembered standing beside him and Eliza and Grove and watching William's father's new white stallion with wistful eyes.

There had been a special bond between the four of them. They were all close in age, all privileged by birth, all blessed with health and exuberance. The two boys had roamed the countryside as if they were young conquerors. Eliza and Fiona, while more restricted because they were girls, had managed to sneak away to be with the boys more than was proper for young ladies of birth. They had shared many good times together.

It was difficult for Fiona to be with William Haversly and not recall those happy days. But any laughter she had shared with him was all in the past, she reminded herself sternly. Her concern was how to deal with Constance. It was to that end that she should bend her thoughts.

The carriage rolled on at a placid pace until they finally reached the house. Fiona bid Mrs. Dyer good night. Then she followed Constance up the stairs and down to the younger woman's bedroom.

Constance pulled the combs from her hair and watched warily.

"Sit down," Fiona said crisply.

Constance obeyed, sitting in a corner chair amid a profusion of white linen pillows.

Fiona remained standing in the center of the room. "You probably think I mean to take you to task for your machinations tonight."

Her sister said nothing. She looked small and innocent with her wide skirts floating out around her. Fiona was not deceived.

With quick, restless steps Fiona paced the large room. "I will not demean myself or you by ranting and raving at you. Neither will I ask you if you had made arrangements earlier to meet James."

The younger woman looked relieved.

Fiona made a tight turn in the center of the room and stalked toward the veined marble fireplace. In the mirror over the mantel she saw her reflection. Her eyes looked wide and bright with strain. Her face was taut. "I shall simply tell you that we shall pack our things and return to Surrey immediately if there is another such incident as the one tonight."

Constance gasped. "You mean *leave* London in the middle of the Season?"

"That is precisely what I mean." Fiona saw her reflection looking rigid and unyielding. Even though no trace of hurt or disappointment showed in her face, she felt it in her heart. She did not want to punish her sister, but she could not permit this liaison to continue. There was too much pain associated with the Haversly family. Even though Papa was dead, there were still Mama and Grove to consider. Each would be devastated to learn that Constance was consorting with a Haversly.

Especially Grove. Even after all these years, he had not recovered from the effects of that duel. Oh, his body had healed, but he had never returned to the laughing, devil-may-care fellow Fiona remembered so fondly. After the duel he had come to display an air of cold calculation that had not existed before.

Repressing a sigh, Fiona brushed back wisps of hair from her forehead. She still remembered how angry Papa had been after William Haversly called to talk with him. That had been right after William returned from the Continent. Fiona never knew what was said, but she did know that immediately after the visit, Papa ordered a new road cut from their house to the main road so he would never have to pass Haversly property again. The families that had once been fast friends became bitter enemies.

Constance's movements brought Fiona's attention back to the present. Skirts billowing, she bounced off the chair. "We cannot leave London, Fiona! It is only mid-April. What about the rest of the Season? What about the party I was to have?"

"The Season will take place without you. There will be no party if we return to Surrey."

"Oh." The word was a miserable whimper. Constance began to cry.

Fiona resisted the impulse to soften at her sister's

tears. Unless she held firm, Constance would continue to practice her charms on James Haversly. This was the only way to end the flirtation before it became something more serious. "Do you understand what I have said?"

"Yes." The word was a pathetic bleat.

"Very well. Good night." Fiona felt no sense of triumph as she closed the door and brushed a weary hand through her hair. It was not her wish to act as taskmaster. On this issue, however, there could be no compromise.

Knowing that she had done the right thing and feeling good about it, however, were two different things. Tension kept her awake much of the night. Although she did sleep fitfully, at dawn's light she was wide-awake and gave up the effort of trying to sleep. Rising, she dressed in a simple green muslin and went quietly down the stairs and out the back door to the small garden behind the house.

The stone bench just outside the door was still wet with dew. She touched it and absently rubbed the moisture between her fingers as she moved into the garden. From the brick kitchen behind the house she heard sounds of activity. Over the low stone wall, she saw a stablehand sweeping out the stalls. A cat outside the stable basked in the first rays of the morning sun.

It would have been a lovely time to write, Fiona thought, if she were not so distracted. Pausing by a bush of pink roses, she plucked a few dead leaves and cupped them in her hand to smell them.

She and Grove had come to this very garden a week after the duel. It had been necessary for two male servants to carry her brother out since he could not yet walk. His color had been good, though, and he had demanded fresh air. He had sat on a chair brought from the dining room.

Fiona thought he was finally well enough to talk about the duel. "What happened, Grove?" she asked. The men who had brought her brother home bleeding and unconscious had given only sketchy details. She wanted to know what had really taken place on that heath in the foggy morning light.

Grove looked away from her. "It is not a matter I can discuss with a lady."

She bent to place the slipping blanket more securely around him. "I am not some missish woman who will have the vapors. You know me better than that."

Grove was silent for a long time. Finally he said slowly, "The quarrel was over a woman. A dancer. William was bitterly jealous because she chose me over him."

Fiona's thoughts should have been entirely for her brother. But a small, guilty part of her thought about William Haversly. When she had seen him in London for the first time turned out in a Bath coat of exquisite cut and a cravat of delicate folds, her feelings toward him had become more complicated. Each time she had spied him at a party or a fete, she had experienced a fluttering, knotting sensation behind her rib cage.

Fiona thought he was not indifferent to her. There seemed something more golden in his smiles toward her, something more intent in his gaze when he spoke with her. He seemed to want to stand up with her as much as he could.

But she must have been mistaken. Else why had he fought a duel over another woman?

Fiona's thoughts came back to the present as she

crumpled the dried rose leaves and let them flutter to the garden path. How absurd to care whether or not Grove and William had dueled over a woman. It was almost as if she were jealous. And of course she was not.

Grove had explained to her that he had tried to reason with his boyhood friend, but William had been beside himself with jealousy. He had fired at Grove before the count was complete. When Grove fell, William left without so much as a backward glance. At every turn, William Haversly had behaved like a cad and a blackguard.

Remembering all that strengthened Fiona's determination to separate Constance from James Haversly. She did not want her sister to associate with anyone whose family lacked scruples.

Chapter 5

WILLIAM WAS sitting in a wing-back chair in his study reviewing a committee report when he heard the front door bang open.

"There now, master, just a few steps to the stairs. Let me help you."

"I can m-make it m'self juss fine," James sang at the top of his voice.

"Shhh. Not so loud, master. It is very late."

"Late! Devil take it. 'Tis the shank of the evenin', Giles! The moon is at its z-zenith. Ever'one should be awake to enjoy it."

William put aside his papers and his glasses and went out into the hall. His brother, looking red-faced, jovial, and very drunk, stood unsteadily in the hallway under a scowling portrait of a venerable ancestor.

"Good evening, James," William said coolly.

" 'S'nice night." He swayed and smiled happily at no one in particular.

William turned to the servant. "Giles, take him upstairs and put him to bed. I daresay he will have an unpleasant reminder in the morning of this night of excess."

The gray-haired servant tightened his grip on his

charge's arm. "Yes, sir, I apologize for Master James's condition."

The makings of a smile worked at the corners of William's mouth. "Why should you apologize, Giles? You have no more control over him than you had over me when I was as young and as foolish a cawker. My recollection is that I, too, sometimes indulged beyond my capacity."

The servant's smile was restrained. "Well, sir, there is that," he said diplomatically.

"Yes, there is that." Feeling less out of charity with his brother, William went back to his study. Through the open door he heard Giles trying to coax James up the steps.

How long ago it seemed since he and Grove had participated in similar nights of revelry. He only hoped James had better sense than he. William's and Grove's youthful indiscretions had not stopped with mere drinking and gaming.

They had been two young bucks intent on their amusement. By the time they had been in London for two Seasons, experience in high society and with the demimonde had made them arrogant and willing to try anything. More than once the two of them had bribed the coachman leaving the Golden Cross to let them take the reins on one of the day coaches to Brighton. William remembered racing with careless abandon, oblivious to the alarmed faces of the passengers. Young and invincible, neither he nor Grove had been troubled by thoughts of the coach overturning. How could it? Even if they reached the outrageous speed of fifteen miles an hour, they could not have had an accident. They led charmed lives. Both he and Grove had been secure in the belief that nothing could go seriously wrong in their world.

After a while, though, the nights of drinking, the painted high flyers, the gambling excesses, and the general recklessness started to seem pointless to William. Slowly he began to rein himself in. Not so Grove. He grew even more daring. He frequented gin houses in the dangerous areas of St. Giles's Rookery—areas where men were knifed in the dark with little provocation.

Looking back, William wondered if there was anything he could have done to stop his friend's flirtation with danger. Would it have helped if he had talked to Grove's father? But the idea of turning to a *parent* for help would have been unthinkable to William at nineteen.

Besides, even though William had tempered his own excesses, he had scarcely become a saint. Yet he had limits. He thought Grove had limits, too. William found out differently the night of the Meredith's ball.

The ball was held on a sticky London night late in the Season.

William and Grove and Manning Stockford had arranged to meet at the ball at the fashionably late hour of midnight. Manning was as rich and idle as Grove and William. Each of them affected a young buck's ennui. Dressed in the first stare of fashion in boots made by Hoby, glossy black top hats made by Lock himself and clothes by Weston, they had money enough in their pockets to gamble away the night. William winced to recall that he had even carried a quizzing glass.

"It is going to be a deadly dull evening," Grove

grumbled five minutes after arriving at the Meredith's overdecorated salon. The three men stood at the edge of the gaudy pink room and disinterestedly watched the dancers. Pretty debutantes glanced at them with obvious interest, but none of the three responded. Although each knew he would someday be expected to choose a wife from these ranks, at the moment, women of easier virtue held more interest.

"We should have gone to the theater to see that black-haired actress, Molly," Manning said.

Grove laughed. "You know very well Molly is in Lord Raney's keeping."

Manning smiled knowingly. "That may be, but I do not think she is particularly devoted to him. I daresay I could have dinner with her after a performance if I wished."

Grove smirked. "Not unless you mean to buy her a good deal more than a meal. I have heard Molly does not come cheaply. She likes her diamond trinkets."

"I have always been generous with my light-o-loves." It was the sort of bragging, self-absorbed bravado that they all indulged in.

William wandered away and left the other two. It did not take long for him to find the gaming tables in a bright blue room down the hall. The Merediths had outdone themselves in here. Naked cherubs looked down on him from the ceiling as he settled into a lyre-backed chair in front of the baize table to indulge in cards and fine liquor.

He was there less than half an hour before Grove appeared and leaned down to mutter, "This party is a damned funeral, Will. What say we go find something more lively?"

The cards had been in William's favor, but the company was dull, and he was bored. "I stand ready to leave. Where is Manning?"

"I left him with someone's wife. Let us say you and I do not seem to be uppermost in his thoughts at the moment."

William did not dally with the wives of other men, but he was not such a stick as to care whether or not another man did. He knew it was the way of society for women to marry for position and then find their amusement or affection outside their marriages.

He finished the hand, pushed back his chair, and rose. He and Grove started down the hall together, their boots sounding loud on the polished floor.

They left the house together. Each had come in his own carriage.

Grove stopped beside his. "I don't feel like trundling about town in a cumbersome carriage like an old woman." His waiting groom was already busy letting down the steps and lighting the sidelights. Grove ignored him.

"Would you rather walk?" William asked dryly.

"No, I have a better idea. Are you game for some sport?"

William shrugged. "I have nothing better to do."

"Then why do we stand here idle? Let us go. Have your driver follow my carriage."

Grove's idea, William soon discovered, consisted of going to a shabby livery stable, rousting the proprietor and his ostler from bed and hiring two nervous-looking pieces of horseflesh.

William watched as the ostler saddled the horses. "So far this idea of yours seems splendid," he drawled sarcastically to Grove. "I can think of nothing better than sloughing about town on those two prancing bits o' blood."

Grove merely looked at him with a superior smile and paid the proprietor.

Once they were saddled on the dispirited nags, Grove dismissed the servants.

William watched his carriage clatter down the cobblestone street and out of sight. "Why did we not go back to our own stables and get some real horses? Or at least go hire a decent horse from Mr. Tilbury?"

"Because we do not want to be recognized."

William heard the edge of excitement in Grove's voice and realized it had been no mere whim to rent these horses. Grove had plans. William, in spite of his pretended boredom and worldliness, was still full of enough youthful spirit to be curious about those plans.

He followed Grove toward the Dover Road. As they passed beneath a street lamp, William glanced at his grinning friend. He could not recall the last time he had seen Grove this excited. It whetted his own taste for whatever was to follow.

Even the horses seemed aware something was afoot and increased their pace accordingly. The two men rode beside each other out the road toward Dover. William did not bother to ask where they were going. It added to the mystery not to know.

The crowded streets and lights of the city gave way to fewer buildings and fewer lights. At length the road continued into darkness.

They must have ridden for an hour and a half before Grove pulled off the road. William followed suit.

Grove tossed something at him; it landed on the horse's neck. "Put that over your face and take off your watch fob and ring. My friend," he announced dramatically, "this may not be Gad's Hill or Bagshot Heath, but I fancy it is a fair enough spot for a robbery. You and I are about to become highwaymen."

William stared into the darkness, trying to see his companion's face. "Are you jesting?"

"I have never been more serious."

"Damnit, Grove, have your wits gone begging? We may not be as respectable as some, but I trust we have not lost all pretense to respectability."

"Don't be such a prig." Excitement rang in Grove's voice. "We are not going to hold up just *any* carriage. Manning will come by here shortly. I'll wager we shall give him something to remember about tonight."

William felt himself relax. For a moment, he thought Grove had been serious about holding up a carriage on the open road, but it was only Manning he meant to scare. "Why the devil would Manning be way out here?"

"He thinks he is going to an assignation at a house down the road with a certain lord's wife. I may have planted that idea in his mind." Grove chuckled. "Can you imagine the expression on his face when he is confronted with two unsavory rogues in masks and riding hungry-looking horses?"

William could not repress a grin. It *would* be a bit of a lark to see Manning's face. They would all get a good laugh out of it tomorrow at White's. Well, perhaps Manning might not see the humor of it, but others would.

"Take off your coat and pull your shirt out," Grove directed. "We do not wish to look like rich nabobs. We must appear disheveled and disreputable. Untie your cravat."

William heard Grove rustling around in the darkness obeying his own commands. He started to do likewise, then paused as a thought struck him. "We do not have a weapon. Manning will laugh in our faces if two men hold him up without a pistol."

"Blast! I hadn't thought of that." After a moment, he decided, "No matter, I can keep my hand beneath my shirt and make him think I have a pistol. Hurry, take off your jacket; I hear the carriage now."

A coach was indeed approaching at a goodly rate of speed. William laughed. "It would appear Manning is most anxious to see his ladylove."

"Yes."

"We move when I give the signal."

They waited beneath the trees in the darkness. William watched the sidelights of the carriage grow bigger as the carriage approached. It was almost upon them before Grove shouted, "Now!" Grove prodded his horse into action. William was right beside him.

The frightened driver whipped blindly at the horses in a valiant but futile effort to escape. Grove easily caught the reins of the lead horse and pulled the carriage to a halt. William spared only a moment to feel sorry for the hapless driver, then his thoughts turned to Manning and the fun they were going to have at his expense.

Grove turned the reins over to William and wrenched open the door. The lights on the side of the carriage revealed a white-faced man huddling in the corner. William's first thought was how odd and aged Manning looked. Then he realized the occupant was not Manning.

By now Grove must have discovered the same thing.

William was ready to spur his horse away when he heard Grove's cold, deliberate voice saying, "Give me your rings, your watch and chain, and your money."

William stared. What the devil was wrong with Grove? Couldn't he see this was not Manning? It was all a mistake, and they must beat a hasty retreat before more harm was done.

"Watch the driver," Grove called over his shoulder. William turned to see the driver sitting rigidly, both hands flung up in the air. When William looked back at Grove, he saw a gun glinting in his hand.

The terrified man in the carriage pulled a large ruby ring from his finger and surrendered it along with his purse. "I have a wife and five children. I beg of you do not hurt me."

"Of course not," William said.

Grove sliced a roughly silencing look at him.

Anger rose inside William. He was not going to be a part of this. He let go of the reins and slapped at the lead horse's rump. The frightened horses darted away. Without the lights from the carriage, he and Grove were thrown back into darkness.

Shaking with anger, William turned to the shadowy form beside him. "Are you completely mad, Grove?"

"We must put our jackets back on and take off the masks," was the calm reply.

William waited in stunned silence as Grove put his clothing to rights. Then he yanked his mask from his own face in disgust.

"It would serve you right if that man went directly to the next town and roused the sheriff."

"He won't," Grove said smugly. "He knows we would be long gone before he can return. Stopping to talk to the sheriff would only delay him. Any man traveling at night does not wish to be delayed."

In silent fury, William turned his horse back the way they had come and started for London. He did not wish to ride beside Grove.

As he pounded toward London, William tried to make sense of it all. He had known Grove since they were both in leading strings. Grove had sometimes lied to a nanny or stolen a small trinket, but those had been childish pranks. There had never been anything in his character to suggest he would rob a man at gunpoint like a gritty Dick Turpin.

An air of unreality lay over the whole event. Grove seemed as calm as if nothing amiss had happened. It almost made William doubt what he had seen. But he *had* seen it. What was more, he had been a part of it. Acknowledging that made his hands nerveless on the reins.

It was a very long journey back. His anger had time to fester.

It was six in the morning before William reached his house in St. James. He walked woodenly through the door and up the stairs. Waving aside the drowsing valet who came to life to assist him, he sank into a dark wing chair and brooded. The damned fool Grove had robbed someone on the open highway. Worse, *he* had been an accomplice.

Jerking up out of the chair, he stomped to the fireplace. He was not some wilting schoolboy who feared adventure, but this was highway robbery, and Grove had dragged him into it. He ought to cut out Grove's liver.

William's hands curved into fists at the memory of Grove holding a gun. What if the man in the carriage had also had a gun? Many people traveling at night carried them. Grove could have gotten them both killed. Or what if the man had panicked and Grove had shot him? William would have been a party to the murder.

William's fury increased as time wore on. The bottle of Scotch he drank to calm himself only made him more volatile. By nine o'clock he was aflame.

William was on Grove's doorstep fifteen minutes later. "He is asleep, Lord Haversly," said the kindly old butler who had known William since he had run tame through the Bailey's house.

"Then I shall awaken him." Ignoring the startled servant, William stalked up the broad, curving stairs to Grove's room.

"Wake up," he shouted.

The other man came out of his sleep groggily. "What the—? Who's hollering? William, it's you. You look bloody awful."

William lunged forward and grabbed him by the collar of his nightshirt. "You bastard, what the hell did you think you were doing last night?"

Grove's puzzled frown gave way to a slow smile. "Ah, yes, last night."

William fought back the inclination to pummel his boyhood friend senseless. They were no longer boys. Neither were they friends. That had all changed last night. "I won't abide this, do you hear me? No man puts me in such a position without suffering consequences. You are the lowest form of life that ever crawled. Name your seconds."

Grove shrugged out of his hold and rose from bed, a bemused expression on his face. "Are you calling me out, William?"

"That is precisely what I am doing."

"Why?"

"Do not insult me with such a question. You know very well why. I will not tolerate being dragged into dishonorable behavior."

Grove scratched at his chest and yawned. "For god's sake, don't act like some missish girl. Be a man. It was all in sport."

"You stole that man's ring and money, Grove. You are nothing more than a common criminal. Pity they don't still hang them in chains at the scene of the crime."

A harder expression came over Grove's face. "I have no doubt you would relish that. But consider that you would hang alongside me. You were there. Your face was also covered." His tone turned nasty. "Since you do not value your health any more than to take a bullet through your chest, I shall be happy to oblige you."

"I rather think it is you who shall take the bullet."

It was bravado on both parts. They had often practiced shooting together, and both knew they were evenly matched. It had never occurred to William he would ever aim a pistol at another living person. He did not even hunt animals. Yet here he was challenging his oldest friend to a duel. "I shall make the necessary arrangements," he said tersely and marched from the house.

The next morning at dawn William stared down the meadow toward Grove. A light fog made everything look ghostly and unreal. A handful of spectators stood nearby, including a doctor and a second for each of the participants. No commands had yet been given.

William was checking his pistol when someone shouted, "Look out, William! He is aiming at you."

He jerked his head up to see Grove's gun directed

right at him. In hindsight, he realized he should have dropped to the ground. But he had been young and nervous and full of self-righteous anger. He had panicked and fired back. Grove dropped to the ground just as a thick blanket of fog rolled over the field.

Chapter 6

FIONA HAD been meaning to visit Lady Eliza for several days. But with the rush of parties that attended Constance's coming out, she had been too busy. She wondered why Lady Eliza had not attended the last few soirees. When Eliza missed the opening night at the theater to see Edmund Kean's Shylock—Lady Eliza loved Shakespeare—Fiona knew something was wrong. She and Constance went the very next day to pay a call, even though they missed a special showing of the private art collection of Lord Radstock.

Upon arrival at the elegant town house, they were shown in by a footman who directed them to a room down the hall. Fiona entered the room and paused involuntarily, startled at how small and wan Lady Eliza looked. She was sitting in a chair by the window in a pale blue room with a small lap rug over her knees.

Eliza beamed when she caught sight of them. "Fiona! How wonderful of you and Constance to come to visit." She did not rise.

Fiona crossed the room and reached out to touch her friend's cheek. It felt hot and dry. "Are you feeling quite the thing, my dear? You look ill."

"It is nothing, only a mild fever. I shall recover and be my old wicked self before you know it."

When she smiled, she almost looked like the old Eliza. Still Fiona was concerned. "Have you been ill long?"

"A short time. I am feeling much better than I was only a day ago." She waved her hand impatiently. "Come, come, we must not spend the time talking about me. What of Constance?" Eliza turned to the younger woman. "Well, my child, I am persuaded you have much to tell me about the Season. I have not attended the last few parties, so I am anxious to hear all about them. We shall have a nice coze and you can tell me who has a tendre from whom and what Lady Jersey wore to the last party at Almack's."

"The parties have all been very nice," Constance said politely.

"What else have you done while in London?" Lady Eliza asked.

"I have gone to the opera. And I went to Vauxhall Gardens four nights ago," she added, her voice trailing off. She looked toward the window.

Lady Eliza frowned. "You do not sound excited. Was Vauxhall Gardens not enjoyable? I recollect that it was a delightful place to flirt from behind one's fan. Do young ladies no longer do such things?" she teased gently.

"Some do," Constance murmured.

Fiona repressed a sigh. If only Constance would give other men a chance instead of pining for James Haversly. Fiona would be glad when her sister was finally over this attraction.

Lady Eliza turned to Fiona with a laugh. "It would seem the debutantes have become blasé. When you and I were seventeen, we were aflutter with the thrill of it all. Do you remember the soiree where the Prince Regent asked you to stand up with him? I thought you were going to faint from the honor."

"You danced with the Prince Regent?" Constance asked with mild interest.

"Yes. It was nothing, really."

"Nothing! Grove and William teased you about it for days afterward. The prince was so dreadfully large you could scarcely get your arms around him. I can still recall William saying that you looked as if—" Eliza broke off and bit her lip. "I am sorry, Fiona, I should not have mentioned William Haversly. But I sometimes forget how it is between the two of you."

"I would rather not talk about him." Particularly not now. He had been on her mind more than she liked. The less she thought about him or talked about him, the better.

Lady Eliza worked her fingers through the soft wool of the lap rug. "It is only that he was so much a part of our youth that it sometimes is difficult for me to see the dislike that exists between you now. We had such fun together, even though William and Grove could make us mad at times. The boys were such friends to each other. Such great friends," she concluded with a sigh of regret.

Constance seemed to be listening with great attention. "Surely if they were once such friends, they could become so again."

"We were all children then," Fiona said briskly. "We were too young to be any judge of character or to recognize William's true nature. William Haversly showed his real self when he shot Grove."

"Naturally I understand why you feel toward him as you do." Lady Eliza looked at Constance before

73

continuing carefully, "It has been many years. For-giveness might be a very healing thing for you."

Fiona stared in surprise. "Have your wits gone begging, Lady Eliza? I have no need of healing. I am perfectly fine."

"Do you think so? I have sometimes thought you hid behind your anger toward William as a way to avoid looking at other things."

"What other things?"

"Your true feelings for . . . perhaps for him."

"That is not at all the case." Fiona pursed her lips and said nothing further. Lady Eliza was not feeling well and could not be expected to think clearly.

The other woman fell silent and looked pensively off into the distance before pulling her light shawl tighter around her as if chilled, although the room was unbearably warm. After a moment, she shook herself and continued, "Where are my manners? I should ring for tea. Could you pull the rope in the corner, Constance? There's a good girl. I have be-come too lazy to even get out of the chair and do my own work."

Fiona was not deceived. She suspected Eliza felt too weak to rise, and the thought alarmed her.

However, once the tea arrived and Lady Eliza sipped at it, she smiled and seemed almost her usual self. Perhaps it was only a passing fever.

She turned to Fiona. "Tell me about the party you are going to have for Constance."

"I am afraid we have been so busy, we have not laid many plans as yet. It will not be too big," Fiona added. "I have never understood parties where there is such a crush that one cannot make one's way through a room."

"Those parties can be dreadfully tedious," Lady

Eliza agreed. "Some hostesses think it adds to their consequence to fill a house to capacity. I do not."

"Well, we shall have enough people to make a pleasant crowd," Fiona said with a fond look at Constance. All the eligible men would be invited so they could see the style with which the Baileys could entertain.

"When is the date?"

"Near the first of June. We shall have to settle that soon. I am waiting to see when the Duke of Bridgewater has his ball; I should not like to place our party opposite it."

"A wise choice."

Lady Eliza's voice seemed to be fading. Fiona guiltily realized they were keeping her from resting. Fiona rose. "I hope you are better soon."

"I shall be back at the soirees in no time." With a smile toward Constance, she added, "You need not fear that the young men will forsake you for me. You are as fresh and pretty as a morning glory. I think their attention will remain on you." Turning to Fiona, she added, "You must come back soon to see me and tell me all about Constance's conquests since she is too shy to do so herself."

Fiona looked at her sister. "There are conquests enough, but I do not think she has settled on any one man yet."

Constance stared mutely at the floor.

Fiona did not doubt her sister was thinking of one man in particular. In time, Constance would forget him and recognize the virtues of one of the many eligible men vying for her notice.

It was after seven in the evening, and still the meeting continued. William sat in the House of Commons, smothering in the overheated, ancient, Gothic building. He could feel the blaze from the candles in the chandelier that hung above the speaker's chair. The stiff wooden bench was uncomfortable, and he shifted around looking for a more agreeable spot. He had no success. He did not care how uncomfortable he was, though, he was not leaving during a discussion this important.

Most of what William was hearing, he already knew. He was aware that power weaving had wrought a change in the cotton and linen mills. Adult males were no longer needed, having been replaced by the cheaper labor of women and children. In some places, the only work for men was carrying their children to the spinning mills to earn the family's livelihood.

Still, those children had homes to return to at the end of their fourteen-hour days. It was the ones under discussion at the moment that tore at William's conscience—the ones being sent to the northern mills by the parish authorities.

"There is nothing wrong with relieving our poor rates by placing the children in honest jobs," the London parish spokesman proclaimed and paused to mop at his brow in the hot room.

William rose. "It is little more than slavery."

Robert Gordon turned from his place near the green baize table bearing the mace to argue patiently. "Come now, William," he began reasonably, "how can you say that when the northern masters have agreed to accept one idiot along with every nineteen sane children? I think they are being more than generous."

William's anger stirred. "These are children, not property." If they are accepting idiots, he thought vengefully, they could start with half the members of the company gathered. But he said instead, "They are still working them like cattle. The masters beat them to make them work even when they are exhausted. Even if the children survive, once they become adults and are too large for the machinery, they are turned off to fend for themselves."

"Really, William, you are making too much of a few instances."

William ignored that and continued. "Even if they are not injured by the machinery, who has not heard of the fever epidemics at Peel's Radcliffe Bridge mills in seventeen eighty-four? These are not healthy places for children."

William had the satisfaction of seeing some men look uncomfortably down at their shoes. Some of the members of the House of Commons employed children in their factories. Before any laws could be passed or conditions changed, they must be made to see the inhumanity of their own actions.

Sometimes, though, he felt as if he were the only crusader. Of course, Peel himself had come to question the factory system, and some mill owners had tried to improve conditions. But until there were laws, the children were not safe.

The debate continued around him. He was hot and tired and irritable. He wished he could go home and relax over a leisurely dinner. Life had been much simpler before he had made this his cause. He could still remember the hedonism of his youth when he cared about nothing but amusing himself.

James seemed set along a similar course at the moment—with one important difference. He had set his sights on a woman of breeding instead of the doxies William had indulged in at that age.

A pity that James's choice was Constance Bailey. Fiona had made her feelings clear on that head. She would never countenance a match between the two young people—not that James might be set on a match. After all, he was young yet. This still might prove to be nothing more than a passing fancy. One thing seemed certain: Fiona's attempts to keep Constance and James apart only fueled their interest in each other. Fiona could not see that, though, and she would never unbend enough to listen to any suggestions he had.

He had a better chance of persuading all the lords and squires and country gentlemen in the House of Commons to reverse their thinking on the child labor issue than he had of making a dent in Fiona's stubborn dislike for him and his whole family.

A few days after her visit with Eliza, Fiona went to the writers' meeting again.

She arrived at Lady Margaret's austere gray parlor precisely at four o'clock dressed in a demure navy gown with a small white ruff at the neck. She carried a few pages of her work. The pages had become so smudged and blotted from working and reworking that she had been obliged to write the whole chapter over.

She smiled at the elderly gentleman already in the parlor by a window. He glanced at her, nodded vaguely, and looked away.

Fiona took a seat on a straight-backed chair and glanced down at her work. The pages were written in a girlishly florid hand. She had tried to make the finishing "s's" leave off meakly, yet somehow they would insist on forming trailing, vinelike endings. The dots over the "i's" would become coy little open circles. It looked absurdly feminine. It was only that in the midst of her writing, the pen flew across the page with a will of its own. Lately this had been even more so than usual. New characters had appeared from the ink of her well without her having preconceived them.

Fiona looked up as Lady Margaret entered the room, an imposing presence in her black bombazine dress. She was followed by two other guests. Shortly afterward a maid appeared carrying a large tray containing tea and bisquits.

Even though it was her second visit, Fiona still felt fluttery and anxious for the meeting to begin.

Lady Margaret, however, seemed inclined toward conversation. Fiona listened while the others talked about important writers on the Continent and about how the war was affecting the delivery of foreign books.

Eventually, the talk turned to politics.

"They say Lord Haversly is quite the rising figure," corpulent Lord Herndon remarked.

"Yes. I understand he gave a fiery speech in Parliament on the working conditions of children," Lady Margaret said. "They say it was very stirring."

Lord Herndon gave a jowly nod. "It is the talk of the ton today. Most impressive."

Fiona listened in silence. She was impressed that William Haversly had taken up such an admirable cause. Straightening in the stiff-backed chair, she reminded herself it was scarcely enough for him to lobby for kindness to strangers when he had been unmerciful toward his oldest and best friend. She wished they would not speak further of William Haversly.

Odd then, that she was the one who asked, "Does

Lord Haversly appear to be winning people to his side?"

"Most definitely," Lord Herndon said. "It will add to his consequence if he does. Who's to say? He might become prime minister one day."

"Not unless he weds," Lady Margaret noted practically. "It would be necessary for a man in such a high position to be married."

"Selecting a wife would be easy enough for him, Margaret," Mr. Richardson joined in. "I'll warrant any of the young ladies being presented this Season would love to make such a catch. For him it is a matter of selecting the one most suited to his social and political needs."

"Indeed," Lady Margaret agreed.

"I should think one of the Palmerman girls would be perfect for him. They are young and lovely, and their father is a powerful force in Parliament."

Mr. Richardson squinted thoughtfully. "I seem to recall Lord Haversly was involved in some unpleasantness a few years back. A duel, I believe. But I doubt it would hurt his chances for a career in politics. After all, he was quite young at the time."

Lady Margaret turned to Fiona. "You are from Lord Haversly's part of the country, are you not?"

"Yes. He—His family lives near mine in Surrey."

"What do the local people think of him?"

Fiona colored. "I do not know." She left it at that. Those present rarely went out socially. They were so absorbed in their books and poems that they failed to keep track of scandals and clearly did not know of the situation between her family and Lord Haversly's. She had no wish to enlighten them. Just speaking about him filled her with anxiety.

She was glad when Lady Margaret finally suggested they critique one another's writing. "Mr. Richardson, why don't we start with you?"

It was hard for Fiona to concentrate once the older man began reading.

Mr. Richardson was followed by Lord Herndon, who read a few short passages from a book he was writing. Then it was Fiona's turn. She read with a nervous catch in her voice. All her carefully turned phrases rang discordantly to her ear as she read them aloud. The more she read, the more her confidence waned. When she was finished, she clutched her papers between her hands and waited.

"It is good," Mr. Richardson said.

Relief ran through her.

"I like the new male character you have added," Lady Margaret said thoughtfully.

Fiona was surprised that the older woman would have noticed a character who had such a small part. "He is only a minor character."

"Really? He seems quite strong and full of purpose. I assumed he was going to play a large role in the remainder of your story."

"No. It's a story about women. I have no plans for a man to play a central role."

Lady Margaret looked at her curiously, then shrugged and brought out her own sheets of paper to read.

Fiona left the writers' meeting an hour later. She was preoccupied with the events of the afternoon and was still reflecting on Lady Margaret's comments when she entered her house and untied her bonnet.

Constance met her in the hallway, her face tear-stained.

"My dear, what is wrong?"

"Lady Eliza has died."

*   *   *

The funeral was simple for one of Eliza's means; her grieving husband explained that she had wanted it that way. Her body was being buried in a church outside London rather than being returned to Surrey.

Fiona felt numb as she sat in the old Tudor church and listened to the service. Mutely, she stared down at her white gloves. Everyone wore white gloves because the deceased was a woman, but everything around Fiona seemed dull and black. A dove that had found its way into the building flew around the vaulted ceiling. Even its cries seemed mournful.

Many people had come from London, and they crowded the old church. Fiona nodded to several people she knew. She even nodded to William Haversly when their eyes met. She was too distracted and full of grief to dwell on her feelings against him at the moment.

In the front of the church, a vicar eulogized Eliza.

"She was a good woman. Always respectful of others."

Fiona's thoughts ranged back to a time when she and Eliza had been girls. She was thinking of their impertinent, smothered laughter behind the nanny's back.

"Lady Eliza never had an unkind thought or did an unkind deed," the vicar continued in a sonorous voice.

Fiona recalled the time she and Eliza had put a shakerful of salt in William's food. She remembered both of them bubbling with laughter over the incident, and she smiled at the memory.

Constance leaned toward her with a worried look. "Are you all right?"

"Yes," Fiona whispered back. Her memories comforted her far more than the eulogy. Lady Eliza had not been a saint, but she had been a good friend, and Fiona would miss her sorely.

"She was full of good purpose and forgiveness toward those who wounded her," he continued.

Eliza had spoken to her of forgiveness the last time they met, Fiona thought. But Eliza had been ill then and not thinking clearly. Besides, it was easier for others to offer advice, but even Lady Eliza had not known the full circumstances. Whenever she asked after Grove, Fiona said that he was fine. But he was not. His life had been altered for the worse by the duel. That made forgiveness impossible.

Fiona was glad when the singing began and she could distract herself with the music.

After the service ended, Constance left with acquaintances to return to London. Fiona stayed behind. She was not quite ready yet to leave. In silence she followed the little band of remaining people around to the back of the church. She could feel the coolness of the damp flagstones through her thin slippers.

A greater coldness came over her when she reached the graveyard and saw the mound of freshly turned earth that marked the site of Eliza's grave.

There was no formal graveside service, but some people offered silent prayers of their own. Others joined hands and stood quietly.

Most of those left were family members. Fiona stood respectfully apart from them. However much she might have loved Eliza, she was not family.

One other person stood separate from the others near Fiona. Out of the corner of her eye she could see the glossy tip of William Haversly's boot. His family had had strong ties with Eliza's family, and he had attended Eton with Eliza's brother.

William walked over to her and bowed. "I offer you my sympathy. I know you and Eliza were good friends."

"Yes," she murmured, unable to look at him.

After a moment, he said, "This is not the first time you and I have attended such a sad event together."

Fiona made no reply. She knew he was referring to the death of her beloved uncle Louis when she was fourteen. The news of her uncle's death fighting the French had hit her like a steel fist in her stomach. She had been young and without knowledge of the "proper" way to handle grief.

Her mother had explained the family must sit in the long, formal living room and receive the visitors who called to offer condolences.

That evening Fiona sat with her family to receive callers. Around her, all was gentle murmurs and polite expressions of sorrow. But hers had not been a quiet grief that could be contained in such surroundings. She felt a restless, searing anger building inside her until she had to escape the stifling confines of the room. She hated Napoleon for waging a war that had cost her uncle his life. She hated the British for allowing her uncle to go so far away to his death. She hated the French for being French.

It was unseemly, she knew, to slip from the house and out the back door. But she cared nothing about seemliness at the moment. Heedless of her fine kerseymere frock, she ran down the steps and into the garden. Vines whipped at her dress as she fled out behind the stables and into the woods. The tears she had held in all day streamed down her face.

Dusk was settling, and in the woods it was almost dark. She did not run far in the woods before she tripped over a tree root. In language completely unbecoming a lady, she collapsed beside the tree and wept bitterly.

It was William who found her. She heard his footsteps as he came through the brush.

"Fiona . . ."

"I *won't* go home," she told him defiantly.

He sat down beside her on the clammy ground. "All right, then."

"And if you say one thing about ruining my gown, I shall never speak to you again."

"The dress doesn't matter."

She rubbed at her cheeks with the backs of her hands and did not look at him.

"It is hard," he said quietly.

Fiona was silent.

"When my mother died, I felt completely isolated. Everyone meant to say the right thing and be helpful, but it did not help."

"No," she murmured.

They sat for a long time, ignoring the cold and the deepening night. Sometimes they did not speak. Other times she raged against the unfairness of death, and he listened wordlessly. When William did talk, it was in a thoughtful, slow voice that sought not to brush away her pain but encouraged her to explore it.

The sound of voices brought Fiona back to the present. She looked up to see William still standing beside her. She wondered if he had any inkling what her thoughts had been. Of course not. However perceptive he may have been toward her at one time, he had changed. All that was sensitive in him as a boy had been left behind.

"Lady Eliza knew she was very ill," he said. "She had known for some time."

"She did not tell me. I went to see her only the other day."

He looked into the distance. "Do you remember how she never could keep a secret as a girl?"

"No, she could not. She certainly changed in that respect."

"We all changed, Fiona."

She sighed. "Yes."

"Maybe none of us for the better. Once the innocence of childhood is lost, people often become strangers to us."

She did not think he was speaking entirely of Lady Eliza. Grove? Perhaps he was implying that Grove would have changed without the duel. He would have changed, she agreed silently, but she did not think he would have become so cold and bitter. But today she did not wish to argue or speak of any unpleasantness. The day was sad enough already.

"It is a chilly day," she said in an effort to make the subject less personal.

"Yes."

Eliza's brother walked up to them, and after a few minutes she took her leave of absence and returned to her carriage.

Although she left William behind, her mind was not clear of thoughts of him. She wished William had not changed. Otherwise, they could still be good friends. Eliza's death left Fiona feeling alone and in need of a friend.

Chapter 7

WRITING WAS a means of solace for Fiona. Through it, she could retreat into her characters and their make-believe world and forget for a while the pain of her good friend's death.

But it was not possible to write all the time. She had social obligations. To shirk them would hurt Constance.

Three days after Eliza's funeral, Fiona and Constance attended a mid-Season ball. James Haversly was there. Fiona was glad he had the decency not to ask Constance to stand up with him. Still, she was not blind to her sister's yearning looks toward the younger Haversly brother.

It was an elaborate event, but Fiona was not in the mood for gaiety. She was glad when the evening ended.

She was up early the next day sitting at her little desk writing with quick, sure strokes. The words flowed. The story was going so well that she was disappointed when Dorothea appeared to tell her it was time to dress to receive visitors.

Rising, Fiona put her hands on the small of her back and stretched tired muscles.

"What would you like to wear today?" the maid inquired.

"My lavender silk, I think."

Fiona was dressed in the simple lavender gown, and her curls were bound with a matching ribbon when she reached the hallway half an hour later. Her cheeks were pink from a fresh scrubbing, and she was feeling cheerful with life.

She felt even better when Lord Borough was announced to see Constance. She had seen him noticing Constance last night, and she had hoped he would call. He was a man of breeding and quiet charm. He also possessed dark good looks and an appealing smile. Any girl in her right mind would be pleased to be taken up by him.

Fiona was relieved to see Constance show some interest in him. The young pair were talking amiably when the butler appeared in the doorway to announce the second caller.

"Mr. James Haversly," he said in sonorous tones.

Fiona felt her jaw tighten. James, looking disagreeably handsome and smiling confidently, appeared in the doorway bearing flowers. His green coat and buff-colored unmentionables were almost the same colors as those Lord Borough was wearing. On James, Fiona hated to admit, they looked better.

"Good morning." He bowed and advanced into the room. "Miss Constance, I have taken the liberty of bringing you these blue flowers as they so reminded me of the color of your eyes."

Constance cast a pleading look toward her sister as if asking what to do. Fiona nodded. What choice had she but to give permission to accept the flowers? To tell James to leave would create an unpleasant scene in front of their other visitor.

While Fiona looked resentfully at James, whom

she was sure must realize her predicament, he smiled steadily at Constance.

The younger woman took the flowers. "Thank you, sir. You are very kind."

There was no fault to find in her sister's acceptance of the gift, Fiona noted, although Constance's cheeks were flushed and her hands trembled.

"Please sit down and join us," Fiona said. The alternative seemed to be for him to stand foolishly for the next hour. James showed no hint he meant to leave.

He settled onto a chair next to Lord Borough. "Good morning, Jonathan."

"Do you two know each other?" Constance asked.

Lord Borough smiled. "Indeed we do. We bloodied each other's noses more than once on the playing fields at Eton. Cricket," he elaborated.

"I was unaware you were an athlete, Lord Borough," Constance said.

Lord Borough laughed. "Not such a one as James here. He was a bruising player. Bang up to the mark, I should say. Of course," he added with a touch of affable smugness, "he was never as good as his older brother William."

"One man's opinion," James commented dryly.

The conversation settled easily into talk of last night's fete. When a third gentleman arrived it developed that he, too, knew James.

There was nothing for it but for Fiona to endure quietly and wait for the visit to end.

Beside her, Constance was radiant. Her conversation was lively, and her laughter freer than it had been for a week.

Fiona sipped at her tea and reasoned with herself. She had not matured to seven-and-twenty without learning that romance is a fleeting thing. Had she not once had a tendre for James's brother? She had certainly gotten over that. Given time, Constance would forget about James.

Fiona set the cup on the tea table and shifted uneasily in her chair. The problem was that she did not have time. The Season would be over in less than a month. Since Papa was dead and there was no male in the family nearby, suitors must apply directly to Fiona for Constance's hand. Two gentlemen had already requested appointments to speak with her. As long as Constance's affection was with James, Fiona knew she would not be able to persuade her to accept any other man.

"It has been very good to see you, Miss Bailey, Miss Constance."

Fiona came out of her reflections to see Lord Borough rising. Smiling, she rose and escorted him to the door. "I do hope you will call on us again," she told him warmly.

"I would consider it an honor." He looked back into the room, his gaze going straight to Constance.

Fiona wished her sister would return his longing look, but she was engaged in conversation with James Haversly.

James Haversly remained less than ten minutes longer, but it felt like ten hours to Fiona. "Good day, sir," she told him in matter-of-fact tones when he finally stood by the door. She extended no invitation to pay a return visit.

"It has been a pleasure, Miss Bailey." He turned toward Constance, who was still seated. "I have enjoyed seeing you again."

Constance cast a worried look at Fiona, as if awaiting permission to reply. "I—I am glad that you came." Then she turned very pink and looked away.

The last caller left a short time later and was scarcely out the door before Constance turned to Fiona, urgency in her voice. "You must believe that I did not arrange for James to come today. It is true I *did* send him a message to meet us at Vauxhall Gardens, but today's visit is as much a surprise to me as to you." Her voice rose plaintively, and she looked close to tears.

"I did not think you had invited him," Fiona said.

"You didn't? Then you will not make us return to Surrey because of this?"

Fiona was silent in the face of her sister's pleas. It would not be fair to punish her sister for James's boldness. But now that he knew he could call with impunity since the presence of other guests prevented her from asking him to leave, she thought he would come again. How was she to deal with that?

Constance leaned forward. "What do you mean to do, Fiona?"

"I am not sure," she said slowly. Whatever she did, though, it must be done quickly. There was too little time left in the Season for Constance to have her feelings confused by James Haversly's attention.

Fiona gave her predicament a good deal of thought. She must keep Constance from making arrangements to see James Haversly, but she could not keep from calling and he knew it. Her only recourse, she decided after much turmoil, was to enlist Lord Haversly's help in the matter. As much as she disliked having to do so, she saw no other choice.

With that in mind, she sent a note 'round to his address. He responded with a message saying he would call the following day.

True to his word, he arrived the next day looking

calm and agreeable. He was dressed well in a navy coat and white pantaloons. His easy poise only made her more agitated.

"Your note suggested it was a matter of some importance."

"It is. Please sit down." Fiona already had a pot of hot tea sitting at her elbow. She had planned this meeting so they would not be interrupted by the comings and goings of servants.

The earl sat in a tapestried chair and waited.

"Tea?" she asked.

He had barely declined before she continued, "My lord, I will speak frankly. I do not have my maid present because I wish to have a confidential conversation with you."

He nodded.

"At my age, of course, I can be alone with a man who is not a suitor without causing gossip." Mentioning the word "suitor" made her feel awkward and she hurried on, "I am certain you know I have a pressing reason for inviting you here today."

"I suspected you had not invited me for the pleasure of sharing tea with me." Dry humor sounded in his drawl. His baritone was rich in the large room.

She continued, intent on her subject, "The matter has to do with Constance and your brother."

"I thought as much." There was an edge to his smile now.

Fiona wore a burgundy dress with a ribbon sewn around the high waistline. She wound and unwound the ribbon on her finger as she spoke. "Your brother called on Constance yesterday." Agitated, she wound the ribbon tighter. "He appeared in my house bearing flowers and looking quite defiant." The memory of his arrogance annoyed her anew, and she paused to aim her gaze squarely on her visitor. "You must know the problem this creates for me. I am perfectly capable of handling my sister, but it is left to you to deal with your brother."

"My brother does not ask for my advice."

Fiona pursed her lips. "One must not always wait to be *asked* before offering advice. I am certain there would be precious little advice given in this world if that were the case." Ignoring the sardonic lift of his eyebrow, she went on, "Surely even you can see how wrong a match between the pair of them would be. Even it if were not for the—the hostile feelings between our families, your brother is unsuitable for Constance."

"Why is that?" he inquired.

She shot him a dark look and then said bluntly, "He seems young and irresponsible."

"He is young. So is your sister. Still, you may be right that they are unsuited."

"Then you must see that we have to do something to discourage their interest in each other."

After a moment's silence, William rose and went to look out the window. "Still raining," he observed mildly.

Fiona could have screamed. She rose. Skirts swirling, she marched over to him. Even as children he had infuriated her by pausing to ponder things that were perfectly obvious. "What are you thoughts, milord?" she demanded.

Turning toward her, he casually tucked a hand into his coat pocket. "Has it ever occurred to you that you are driving these two young people together by trying so hard to keep them apart?"

"No." Unblinking in the face of his steady gaze, she demanded, "Do you have a better idea?"

"Yes."

Fiona was so caught up in her anger, she had not noticed how close they stood until she felt his warm breath on her cheek. She stepped quickly away.

"Constance and James should be allowed to see each other."

"That is a ridiculous suggestion." She stalked back to her chair.

William held up an imposing hand. "Hear me out, Fiona. Your impatience was always a fault."

That pushed her to silence even if it did raise her temper.

"Constance is bound to see all the failings in my brother that are so clear to you. You have told me how smart your sister is. Surely such a clever girl will recognize these failings in time."

"I am persuaded she would," Fiona retorted, "but I do not have an unlimited amount of time. We must put an end to this infatuation before the Season is over and her chances for a suitable match elsewhere are ruined."

William sat down again. This time he did not take the chair across the room from her but the one beside her. "You must consider the other side. If James were to spend time with Constance, he might discover your sister is no paragon and give up his pursuit of her."

Fiona stared resentfully. How dare he imply Constance was less than perfection? "I do not know how I ever persuaded myself I could have an intelligent conversation with you. It is apparent you are not going to be helpful in the least."

"On the contrary, Fiona, I do mean to be helpful."

How good he has become at acting, she thought. He almost sounded sincere.

"These are young people who do not yet know their minds," he continued. "But I can assure you that James's attention never remains fixed for long. I think if you had not made this such a challenge, he would already have moved on to another chit."

"I would not be fulfilling my duty if I put my sister in the way of your brother," she informed him icily. "Being in his company is the worst possible way for her to put this infatuation behind her."

William tilted his head to one side and asked curiously, "Pray, enlighten me, Fiona. What is an infatuation?"

"It is a passing fancy. It is thinking one wants another person when one really does not even know that person at all."

"Have you ever had an infatuation?" The words were low, inquisitive, almost sensual. The grayness of the day played in his eyes and made them an even more striking shade of pewter.

His question was impertinent. Yes, she had had infatuations. One of them, foolishly enough, had been for William Haversly himself. But she had been too young then to realize that a quickened heartbeat meant little. "We are not here to discuss my affairs, milord," she said crisply.

"No," he said reasonably, "but we are talking about the dreams of other people. I thought if you reflected on your own dreams it might give you a better understanding into what Constance is feeling."

"I know my sister well enough." She was not going to admit to him that lately she had not been sure she knew her sister at all.

"Do you?" His long, considering look discomfited her.

"Yes, I do." Suddenly restless, she began to roam the room.

He sighed. "I do not wish to upset you further. I am only saying the effort you have made to keep Constance and James apart has failed. Why not try another strategy? If James and Constance do not see each other as forbidden fruit, the charm may fade."

"What if you are wrong?"

"Fiona," he was very serious now as he leaned toward her, "has it ever occurred to you that you cannot control your sister forever? This may be more than an infatuation. They may have fallen in love. If that were the case, then their feelings would be of far greater importance than your wish to keep them apart. I would personally fight you to see that they are together if they were in love."

She faced him, bosom heaving. "You are insufferable."

"And you, Fiona, have forgotten what it is to be young and full of dreams and romance. A pity, for you once had dreams of your own in abundance. You confided some of them in me."

How dare he speak to her of secrets she had shared with him in happier times and under other circumstances? She blushed to think she had once told him of her desire to be a mother to a houseful of children.

"Lord Haversly, I asked you here to discuss a problem, not to reminisce over other times." She felt tense, ready to snap. "Pray, indulge me by concerning yourself with the matter at hand."

"I have made my recommendation." He rose. "Since it has only served to annoy you, I shall take my leave. I believe my staying will only perturb you further. Give my regards to your sister."

"Is it—" Fiona was interrupted by a scream in the hall, which was followed by a short expletive and a heavy crash.

They both started toward the door. Lord Haversly reached it before she did. Fiona rushed after him.

She arrived in the foyer to find Mrs. Dyer and half a dozen servants standing about. Two of the upstairs maids peeped over the balcony like curious schoolchildren.

Fiona's gaze went to the man sprawled in the middle of the floor. The coachman's sticklike legs formed a V as he sat on the floor looking bemused. His face was red and he reeked of rum.

"What the devil . . . ?" Lord Haversly began.

"Mr. Sanders is drunk, milord. He broke that pretty little vase," Mrs. Dyer pointed to porcelain pieces strewn across the slate floor.

Fiona stepped forward. "Go get someone from the stables and have them carry him down there."

A maid scurried off to obey the order.

Fiona turned to Lord Haversly, embarrassed. "I apologize for this. I assure you it is not in the ordinary way of things in this household."

He made no reply, but his expression was one of concern.

Fiona turned back to the others. "You may all return to your chores."

Reluctantly, the excited servants melted away. Two men arrived from the stables and departed carrying the coachmen between them. That left Fiona and William standing in the hall together. She was mortified by the incident and the fact that he had witnessed it. She wished he would leave.

However, he seemed inclined to linger. "Fiona, I know it is difficult for a woman to manage a household alone."

"I do very well."

"Yes." The softness in his voice was as disturbing

as if he had contradicted her. "Still, there may be times when you require a man's help. I know you do not think of me as a friend, but if you ever need assistance, you can call on me."

"Thank you for your offer," she said stiffly. Of course, she would never make use of it.

"It is not fair that you should be in this position," he continued, his voice husky with intensity. "Grove should be here to help you."

She took offense immediately. "You of all people have no right to criticize Grove. He is—"

He cut in angrily. "Fiona, leave off defending him and look at him honestly. He has all but abandoned your family. Your mother's health is frail. You are in London alone trying to launch a sister and maintain a household. You do not even have help in disciplining the servants."

"That is my concern and not yours." It had hurt her that Grove had not responded to the letter she had written to him telling him of Eliza's death, but she was not going to show William Haversly that she had any disappointments about her brother.

He looked hard at her, as if on the verge of arguing. Then he thrust his hands into his pockets and stepped away. "Very well, I will leave the matter alone. You did not call me here to discuss Grove. Your concern is for Constance. If you truly want to do what is best, at least promise to think about what I have said about letting the two see each other."

"I will think about it." Lifting her skirts, she stepped over the broken porcelain and walked to the door in a pointed invitation for him to leave.

He followed.

After the door closed behind him, Fiona stood for a long while beside the door. She had been wrong to ask William Haversly here. Instead of showing him the error of his ways, he had opened the door for her to doubt her own handling of the situation.

But he was right to say she did not have anyone she could turn to for advice. With Mama in Surrey and Grove in Cornwall, she had to rely solely on her own judgment. What if she was wrong and William right? What if she made the situation worse by trying to stand between the two? She wished Eliza were here to help her make a decision. But there was no one, and that made her feel very alone.

Chapter 8

LATER THAT afternoon, Mrs. Dyer sat across from Fiona in the sitting room at the back of the house. Constance was in a corner putting a pretty edging on a handkerchief. Fiona told her sister of her decision. "Mind you," she concluded, "I do not encourage James Haversly calling on you, but I will not try to prevent it."

Constance blinked in amazement. "Truly, you are giving your approval for James to call here?"

"Yes." She prayed she had reached the right decision.

"How splendid." The younger woman beamed with delight.

"I trust I need not remind you you will be receiving other callers. I expect you to show them every courtesy." Fiona also intended to invite the most eligible men to the party she was going to give for Constance. She intended to entertain with taste and elegance. That would not only impress suitors, but their mothers and sisters. Those good women often had much to say in their son's and brother's matrimonial choices.

"Of course." Constance's needlework lay forgotten in her lap.

"And at fetes and soirees you must not show James

Haversly any marked attention," Fiona continued.

"I will not," her sister avowed earnestly.

"I hope not," Fiona said to herself. Constance was already flitting out of the room.

Mrs. Dyer smiled approvingly. "I believe you have done the right thing. Young Constance has been very quiet and unhappy these past few days. I shall be glad to see her smiling again."

"It will be more pleasant," Fiona admitted. She did not like to see her sister sad either. "But I must stress how important it is that we make other callers feel welcome."

Once Constance really looked at some of those other men, she was bound to come to her senses. How could she not? Lord Borough was far too handsome and rich for any girl to resist him long. There were several other men with good looks and heavy purses to recommend them.

Mrs. Dyer smiled serenely and worked at her tatting. "I am persuaded she will soon have an offer she wishes to accept."

"Yes." Once an eligible man captured Constance's attention, the purpose of coming to London would be achieved. Constance would marry and become the mistress of a grand household on some wooded estate.

"After she is married, you can return to Surrey and resume your quiet life." Mrs. Dyer paused to select another color of thread from the basket beside her.

Fiona watched absently. Resume her quiet life, she thought with a touch of misgiving. Would she be happy back in Surrey? Although she had been reluctant to leave there to come to London, now the thought of returning to the big manor house seemed lonely. It would only be her and Mama. Once Mama died, Fiona faced a future alone. All she would have were occasional visits to see Constance.

The thought upset her. Abruptly, she rose. "I believe I shall go to my room and try to write."

"Of course," Mrs. Dyer said pleasantly.

Writing would soothe her anxiousness and put things in perspective, Fiona consoled herself. She was feeling melancholy because of her disturbing visit with the earl. Also weighing on her mind was the task that awaited her of speaking with the coachman.

Of course, she could ask the butler to do so, since he was the one in charge of the servants. But the butler had been unable to stem the coachman's drinking thus far. It was time she confronted Mr. Sanders herself.

Once in her room, Fiona sat at her desk and pulled out a fresh sheet of paper. Where had she left off writing? Ah, yes, the servant had just announced the arrival of the dowager duchess.

Fiona dipped her pen into the inkwell. At first it was hard to concentrate, but she forced herself to write. Soon, ideas and words flowed. She had completed eight full pages before her aching hand forced her to stop.

She rubbed at her wrist and reread the first page. It was good, she decided, but something bothered her. She read the page again before the answer came to her: the man she had intended to be no more than a casual character had already said several things. He had even made a witty remark. Fiona frowned. There was something familiar about him.

She turned to the next page. Lady Margaret was right about this man figuring strongly in the book.

Absently brushing the feather end of the pen across her lips, she leaned back in the chair. What to do? She would have to edit these pages and pare down the man's role. She must make certain his thoughts and feelings did not become central to the story. After all, she was the author and she was in control of this book.

Why had this man become so central anyway? His presence made her both excited and uneasy. It was the same feeling she got whenever she was around Lord Haversly.

With one swift movement, Fiona pushed back her chair. She would not write anymore today. Not if it put her in mind of the earl. He was the last person in the world she wanted to think about.

Lord Haversly was reflecting on his conversation with Fiona earlier that day when he entered White's. He nodded diffidently to the dandies standing in the bow window and went into the reading room. He wanted nothing so much as a quiet sip of bourbon and a chance to read the paper.

He had just sat in a deep chair and leaned back to cross his legs when another member approached.

"Good evening, William."

"Hello, Martin." William tried to keep the tightness out of his voice as he looked up at Lord Kitchmer. The newcomer's family owned a mill in Birmingham and employed hundreds of children to work in it. William's fight to change the child labor laws would have serious consequences for Kitchmer.

"Still preaching insanity?" Kitchmer asked with a nasty smile. He sat down across from William. He was a short, squat man in his early fifties whose buttons strained to keep his waistcoat together.

"No, I preach only decency and concern for those who cannot speak for themselves."

Kitchmer laughed. "You are making a fool of yourself, William. You may give pretty speeches in Parliament that appeal to the masses, but you do not do your own kind any favors. Why do you want to cause an undue burden to the rest of us?" he asked reasonably.

"Because using children for cheap labor is wrong." He put his newspaper aside and looked squarely at Lord Kitchmer.

His companion shook his head. "You could not be more mistaken. We do those children and their parents a favor. We give them money to buy food and clothing. They would starve without us."

"Whereas with you they die or become cripples in your mills tending your looms. The country was far better off when weavers lived in their own cottages and laid their webs of linen to bleach on the grass or spread them on the hedges."

Lord Kitchmer laughed. "You are not before Parliament now, so you needn't read me a speech. The power loom is the greatest invention in history. Those children are blessed that we give them a job manning it."

William bit back further angry words. What did one say to someone who permitted children below the age of seven to work in dangerous conditions? Such a man was beneath contempt. Except that there were so many like him that the demand for children exceeded the supply. Guardians of the poor in London sent little boys and girls to mill owners in manufacturing towns by the bargeful. "Any man with a conscience would not do what you are doing," he finally said tersely.

Deep laughter came from the opposite chair. "And you have a conscience? Come now, William, do not be such a prig. Or should I say a hypocrite? Your own life has been far from a Bible verse. Some may have forgotten, but I know that you shot a man and fled the country. I daresay Grove Bailey does not sing your praises."

"He may not, but we were both men who agreed to a duel. We were not defenseless children who had been whipped by your overseers because we were too exhausted to work."

"So anything you have done is excusable," Kitchmer taunted. "Shooting a man before the signal is given is excusable?"

William was silent. It would be pointless to try to explain what had really happened. Kitchmer would never believe him. Besides, William would not demean himself by trying to gain this man's respect. It was something he could live without.

"If you will excuse me, Martin, I find I no longer wish to remain in your company." He sat forward on the edge of the chair ready to leave, the paper in his hand.

"Is that what the elder Miss Bailey said to you when she turned on her heel and left you standing alone at the Melbourne party? One had the distinct impression she disliked you."

Mention of Fiona touched a nerve and made his words even sharper, "Fiona Bailey has leave to like or dislike me. People's opinions of me are not what matters. The issue is justice for children who have been mistreated by you and by people like you."

"You are a model to us all," Kitchmer said sarcastically. "Do you also mean to call me out and shoot me before I am prepared as you did Grove Bailey?"

"Do not tempt me." William had the gratification of seeing Kitchmer flinch. Without another word, William rose and walked away.

It was not the first time an enemy had thrown his past up to him. It was also not the first time he wished the duel had never happened. He wished Grove had never involved him in a robbery.

But all those were futile wishes. All that had happened, and he could do nothing but go forward. It would help if his family and the Bailey family could reconcile. He had even had a faint hope at the beginning of the Season that that might be possible. Now he knew it would never happen.

Any young woman being launched needed to have a party that was entirely in her honor. Such events offered even plain girls the chance to be the unrivaled center of attention. Constance certainly did not need a party of her own in order to be the focus of masculine interest, but it was still an opportunity to show the world her family's consequence.

A full-scale ball seemed unnecessary since Constance was not the daughter of a duke or marquess. After much consideration, Fiona finally decided that a lavish party with a midnight supper would be appropriate. Fiona was inspired to make the event even more tastefully grand with the intention of attracting other suitors.

It was not that Constance had lacked for proposals. On the contrary, several gentlemen had asked for Constance's hand. None, however, had been acceptable to Constance. Fiona did not press her.

Meanwhile, James Haversly continued to call with irritating regularity. One had only to look at the translucent radiance on Constance's face each time he was announced to feel discouraged.

The thing to do, Fiona resolved, was to prompt other men into action. A splendid party might do that. Surely once the right suitor came up to scratch, Constance would come to her senses.

"I have decided you should have a particularly elegant party," Fiona informed her sister as they were on their way to the linen draper's shop. "You know I have been laying plans for a party for some time, but I would like to make the event even more elaborate. It will require work to enlarge it, but not an overwhelming amount."

"I should be glad to help in any way I can."

Fiona smiled at her sister. Constance had become her sweet-tempered self over the past few days. "Thank you, dear, but a girl in the midst of her Season has better things to do than worry about flowers and silver and menus."

"I want to help," Constance insisted. "I would feel guilty if all the trouble fell on your shoulders when the party is for my benefit."

Fiona leaned across the carriage seat and gave her sister's hand a squeeze. "How generous of you. Very well, if you wish to help, you could write the invitations." That would not take long, and Constance had exceptionally neat handwriting.

"Anything."

Over the next week, Fiona was glad that Constance was taking care of the invitations. Fiona discovered that planning a London party was more of an undertaking than she had supposed. While she had arranged soirees at home in Surrey, those had been for small numbers of local people.

Nearly two hundred people were to be invited for

Constance's party. Those people had spent the last several weeks of the Season at parties where hostesses vied to outdo one another in lavish preparations. They were certain to measure Constance's party with critical eyes, and Fiona was nervous about that. She wanted everything to be perfect for Constance's sake.

Planning the event became as formidable a task as preparing an army for an invasion. There were a thousand tiny details to attend to. Fiona walked around with a notebook attached to her wrist like a dance card. She frequently jotted reminders to herself on it. She was immersed in menu plans, consultations with the housekeeper over linens, overseeing the cleaning of the house. Wherever she went in the house, servants flitted about cleaning floors, lamps, and furniture.

For the midnight dinner, it was necessary to make arrangements to have tables set up in the garden, the drawing room, the dining room and several antechambers. Fiona scarcely had time to order a gown made for the evening, and it was impossible for her to attend the writers' meeting.

When Constance offered to take care of seating arrangements, Fiona gladly accepted. Even Mrs. Dyer was busy helping embroider pretty little name cards for each of the guests.

In the days before Constance's party, there were still routs and fetes to attend, dressmakers to meet with, and teas to attend. Men continued to call, James Haversly among them, and Constance continued to smile prettily and laugh gaily.

Fiona was so distracted by plans for the party, she paid little attention to James Haversly.

The morning before the party, Fiona stood in Hatchard's bookstore gazing blankly at the spines of the volumes and wondering whether she had reminded the chef to purchase fresh strawberries for the syllabubs.

"Fiona?"

She blinked. Lady Margaret stood before her.

"You seemed to be in your own world. I sometimes am that way myself when I think about my writing. A bookstore is a good place to reflect on writing, I find."

She smiled faintly. "I must own I was thinking about strawberries instead of my book."

"Oh. Well, you missed a good meeting Wednesday. Everyone had something to read."

"I wish I could have been there, but I have been very busy."

"Writing, I hope. I was afraid we might have discouraged you with our suggestions."

"Oh no, I am far from discouraged. I mean to return to my story as soon as I can." She had not written on it since coming to the realization a William-like character had invaded the book. But when she had the chance, she would strike that character out.

"Excellent. I am anxious to hear more of your book. You had added that new character who brought such life to the pages."

Fiona winced inwardly.

"Well, I have not much time today. I am glad I saw you, Fiona." Lady Margaret swept away.

Fiona made her purchase and left. Forget about the story and William Haversly, she told herself firmly. She had more than enough on her mind as it was.

The next day was the day of the party. Fiona awoke in a state of nervousness and remained that way all day long. There were so many last-minute details. She hurried back and forth all day seeing to first one item and then another. She was checking the flowers in the center of the main table when Mrs. Dyer appeared.

The chaperone was dressed in a dark blue gown with a lace collar. "It is getting late, Fiona. You should change into your gown. The guests will begin arriving shortly."

Fiona glanced down at her brown muslin dress and then up at the clock. Dear heavens. It was past seven o'clock. "You are right." She hurried upstairs to change into the high-waisted purple gown that had been delivered from the dressmaker just this morning.

As Dorothea helped her into it, Fiona looked into the cheval glass and frowned. The little ribbons that were tied around her neckline and floated over the caps of her white shoulders had looked splendid in the fashion plates. On her, however, she worried that the effect was too youthful.

"Do I look all right, Dorothea? The dress does not make me look as if I am trying to be a debutante, does it?"

"Not a bit of it. It is very pretty and graceful. You look beautiful. I should be surprised if you did not outshine Miss Constance."

Fiona laughed. "At my age! Do not be ridiculous. Men scarcely know that I exist."

"They will when I am through styling your hair," the maid promised.

Fifteen minutes later, with her hair done in a fetching Grecian style, Fiona hid her anxiousness behind a serene smile and stood at the door greeting the first guests. Beside her, Constance looked lovely in a white frock with a blue bow tied just below her bosom.

The first to arrive were the Dorseys. Shortly after came the Bennets. Sir Katlin came looking very distracted. As he handed his beaver hat to the footman, Fiona thought there must be truth to the rumor his pockets were deeply to let and that he would have to leave the country to flee his gaming debts. Lord Borough arrived and bestowed a warm smile on Constance. People were crowding into the house by the time James Haversly sauntered in. Fiona repressed a sigh at the sight of him. She had known her sister would invite him, but she was still disappointed to see him.

The arrival of another promising suitor reassured Fiona. She flashed her brightest smile and turned to the next person. Her smile died.

William Haversly stood in the doorway, his gold-tipped cane was tucked beneath his arm. He wore a gray coat, buff unmentionables, and a crisply-tied cravat. His hair had been cut short and was brushed à la Brutus. He looked dapper, elegant, unsettling. Fiona stood mute. If she had thought about it, of course she would have realized that Constance might invite him. But she had been so busy that she had not thought about it.

Seeing that people were waiting behind him, she forced a polite expression. "Good evening, Lord Haversly."

"Good evening, Miss Bailey."

Even though he was impeccably dressed, he looked tired. That must be from long nights of writing speeches. Not that it mattered to her, of course.

William turned to speak to Constance, and she

found herself facing a cheerful older couple. "How is the new grandson?" she recollected to ask.

"The best new marquess in the world. Scarcely cries at all."

"How nice." Her glance strayed back toward her unexpected guest. She was glad Grove was not here to witness this. He would be angry to know that she was entertaining William Haversly as a guest in her house. Added to that, nothing had been gained by allowing Constance and James to see each other. Their interest in each other had not dimmed as William had led her to hope that it would.

The arrival of other guests pulled Fiona back to her duties as a hostess. But she resolved that after tonight she would forbid Constance to see James Haversly. If her sister would not accept any other offers for her hand, than she would have the coming fall and winter to reflect on her obstinance. Next year, Fiona would bring her back for a second Season. By then she would surely prove more tractable.

Chapter 9

By the time Fiona made her way outside, the musicians had already begun to play in the pavilion that had been set up in the garden behind the house. Those guests too old or disinterested to dance settled into comfortable corners in the house to catch up on the latest on-dits. Others had already repaired to the library to try their hand at faro.

Fiona wandered outside and sat down beside the dowager duchess of Lancaster.

"Are you nervous, child?" the old woman asked.

"Yes."

"Of course you are. Do not be. Things are going tolerably well, though, even if the musicians are out of tune."

Fiona was alarmed. "You think they are playing badly?"

"They are too loud and too tinny. I shouldn't worry about it, though. People forget all about such things in time." She got to her feet, leaning heavily on a cane. "Have a wonderful time, dear."

She left, leaving Fiona to listen carefully to the musicians. Did other people think the playing was bad? There were not many couples dancing, she fretted. Perhaps everyone found the music unacceptable.

"Fiona, there you are." She was drawn into a conversation with some of the guests and spent the rest of the evening talking to people and making frequent visits to the kitchen to check on the progress there.

At midnight the announcement for dinner was made. Fiona stood in the dining room and looked around anxiously as guests found their seats. Constance had arranged the table seatings, and Fiona had had little time to do more than make a cursory check of the arrangements. She thought, though, they were well arranged. The right people were seated at the heads of the tables, and it appeared that diplomacy had been applied in assigning who was seated next to whom.

That left Fiona free to worry about other things. Were the flowers still fresh? Would the food be good?

She was relieved to find the first course of white soup delicious. Around the table and at the adjoining tables, the guests seemed to be enjoying themselves. At the end of her table, she saw Mrs. Bennet laughing companionably at something Lady Findley had said. Lord Borough smiled at Constance. James Haversly was seated across from Constance. At the moment he was talking with someone else, Fiona was pleased to note.

Lord Haversly, she was glad to see, was seated a distance from her, although he was at her table. He conversed quietly with the distinguished Lord Curtin.

Fiona was just beginning to relax when suddenly she heard the burr of dissent amid the gentle hum of conversation and the clink of silver on china.

"We most certainly did not *steal* a servant from your household, Mrs. Jamison. One of your maids may have resigned your household to come to work for us, I do not recall. I take leave to tell you, though, that there is constant unhappiness among your servants. Everyone knows that."

"My servants are the most loyal and content in the kingdom. That you would suggest . . ."

Fiona bit her lip. The two dowagers seated next to each other were sisters by marriage. They could spend entire evenings at parties talking amiably between themselves. They could also, Fiona belatedly remembered, bicker endlessly when the mood was upon them.

Tonight the mood appeared to be upon them.

The other guests politely ignored them. Fiona tried to do the same. She was relieved when their voices subsided during the entrée of larded sweetbreads and rissoles. However, during the second course of garnished brussels sprouts, a flare-up occurred.

"I *never* entertained Emma Hamilton at my house after the scandal. I would not have done anything so improper." Mrs. Jamison blinked indignantly, a brussels sprout slipping unnoticed off her fork, over her bosom, and onto the floor.

"I am certain that you did."

"Never! She was not received in proper circles once she and Lord Nelson became, well, involved. You know that. I would not have had her at my table, and there's an end to it."

Fiona glanced toward Constance, who was looking at her helplessly. "I did not know it would be like this when I seated them near each other," she whispered. "They are going to ruin everything." Her eyes were bright with the makings of tears.

Fiona sketched a comforting smile. "Never mind.

Everyone seems to be enjoying themselves in spite of the dowagers." It was true. Even though she was tense, conversation flowed among the other guests. Here and there she noted a particularly pink cheek—testimony to the power of wine to aid in amusement. Voices were growing a bit louder and more gregarious with the passing of the hours. It was almost one in the morning before the final serving of rhubarb tarts arrived. By then, even Fiona had grown less tense about the friction between the dowagers, and Constance was once again smiling.

Then, abruptly, things got worse.

At precisely one in the morning, Lord Lanton turned to Sir Geoffrey.

"Damn fine woman you are married to, Geoff, what say? A woman who knows how to please." He gave a coarse, drunken laugh. "Yes, sir, she knows how to please a man in the bedroom."

Sir Geoffrey, who was also deep in his cups, threw out his ample chest and demanded, "Pray, what do you mean by that?"

Lord Lanton attempted a wink but in his foxed state ended up blinking owlishly. "I think you take my meaning well enough."

Sir Geoffrey's chest puffed out even further. "You insult me, sir."

The rest of the room had fallen silent. The guests watched the two men and awaited further developments. Fiona gripped the table as she looked around helplessly.

Salvation came from genial Mr. Ludlum who was seated beside Sir Geoffrey. "Sir Geoffrey, why don't you and I step outside and smoke a cheroot? Bit stuffy in here, do you not think?"

Sir Geoffrey shrugged off his neighbor's hand and

snapped, "I am not going outside. Not until I get to the bottom of Lanton's insinuations."

"Oh, dear," Fiona murmured under her breath. Even the dowagers listened raptly. She looked over to see Constance sitting rigid and crimson-faced.

Sir Geoffrey pushed back his chair and rose unsteadily. "I think you should step outside with *me*, Lanton. We have things to settle."

There was a quick shuffling of chairs as other men jumped up and interposed themselves between the two combatants. "Come, come, Geoffrey. You would not want to do anything rash," someone advised.

"I'll see you in hell, Lanton, if you think you can suggest things about my wife."

"Calm down, Geoff, I am persuaded it is all a misunderstanding," some well-meaning person temporized.

Sir Geoffrey's wife quietly sobbed into her napkin.

Lord Lanton was hustled toward the front door over his loud protests.

"Excuse me," Fiona murmured to no one in particular. Rising, she hurried after the group. Someone thrust Lanton's coat into his hands. Fiona ordered a servant to bring his carriage.

She had a vague awareness that Sir Geoffrey had been taken back to the kitchen, probably for sobering coffee. Or maybe so that he could be taken out the back door.

Fiona returned to the dining room to find the rhubarb tarts sitting untouched. All of the guests sat in silence. Many of them watched her.

Fiona looked around helplessly, trying to think of some way to revive the pleasant atmosphere that had reigned before supper. She could think of nothing.

Constance's party was clearly over. Already

guests were beginning to rise. Fiona could just imagine the gossip that would take place in the carriages on the way home and in salons all over London tomorrow. The gossips would conclude that the hostess was at fault for the altercation. "Didn't she *know* Lord Lanton and Sir Geoffrey's wife were just ending a dalliance?" Of course, Fiona had a vague recollection of having heard, but she had not remembered when she saw that they were seated next to each other. Still, it had been Fiona's responsibility to *know* these things and to make certain just such an incident as this one did not take place.

Fiona looked at Constance and saw her sister sitting rigid and devastated. She did not rise, although most of those around her rose to make hasty exits. Fiona watched Lord Borough push back his chair. James Haversly looked sympathetically at Constance but seemed not to know what to say. He, too, left shortly. Constance escaped upstairs.

Fiona stood by the door and exchanged parting words with the guests with as much dignity as she could for as long as she could.

The last guests were gathering shawls and hats when she escaped back to the kitchen. Leaning against a cool wall, she put her hands over her eyes. The evening had been a fiasco. Constance's chance for a perfect match may have died in the embers of the evening. All of the ton put great stock in avoiding scandals. To have two men come to dagger's drawing in one's dining room left a very black mark on the Bailey family. Poor Constance.

William watched the final guests depart. Beaver hat in hand, he stood by the door. Why hadn't he followed his instincts and declined the invitation when it arrived? But he had been curious. He had thought this might be Fiona's way of trying to open the doors between them again. He even thought she might have decided Constance and James might have a future together and that, consequently, she should concern herself with mending fences with him.

There were other factors that had entered into his decision to come. It had been a difficult week, and he knew that even harder battles lay ahead in Parliament. He wanted to go somewhere and relax. He wanted to be among friends. Of all the invitations he could have chosen from this evening, this one had pulled at him the most strongly.

As soon as he entered the house, though, he realized he had made a mistake. Fiona had shown no pleasure in seeing him. Had he somehow hoped that she would? If anything, she had seemed surprised to see him.

It would have been easier for him to slip away if the party had not degenerated into such a disaster. If things had gone normally, he could have murmured a few insincere words to her and vanished. As it was, he must take a more formal leave. He could not leave without a word of parting.

Sighing, he approached a distracted-looking maid. "Where is Miss Bailey?"

"In the kitchen, sir." She pointed.

As he walked down the hall, he cursed his decision to come. He pushed open the swinging door and stepped into the black-and-white tiled kitchen. Fiona stood by a sideboard with a crumpled handkerchief pressed to her mouth. Her eyes were red from crying.

"I have come to thank you for the evening," he said stiffly.

She clutched the handkerchief tighter and looked

as if she wanted the floor to swallow her. "It was a dreadful evening." She looked girlish, vulnerable, greatly in need of consolation.

It *had* been a dreadful evening, but he knew she did not want to hear him agree. He tried for a more reassuring note. "I should not worry. These things are soon forgotten, you know."

"I wanted everything to be perfect." Fiona seemed to speak more to herself than to him, so he did not reply.

But when she looked miserably down at the floor and began to cry softly, he was unable to remain aloof. He stepped closer. "It was only a party, Fiona. The defeat of Napoleon did not hinge on tonight."

She did not move away. Small hands twisting at the handkerchief, she said, "No, but Constance's future hinged on tonight. I have ruined her."

"Would you want a man for your sister who is so weak of spirit he flees when things do not go well?" he asked reasonably.

Fiona looked up at him, a mist of tears making her eyes glimmer. "They are peers," she objected.

"They are men first. Even a royal duke is without recommendation if he has not good character. Honesty and loyalty are of far greater value than money and rank."

"That all sounds very noble, but even you realize Constance's chances were hurt tonight."

William looked down at Fiona's upturned face. She was no longer crying, but her face was still etched with sadness. He could not lie to her. "It complicates things," he admitted. "But she is young and beautiful. And there is next Season."

"Perhaps. But she may never return to London. I never did. She may end up on the shelf like me."

"You have chosen this life, Fiona. Any number of men would have been grateful to have you for a wife. I recall how many men courted you when you were in London." He had been among them. Did she remember that?

Just then the door swung open and the chaperone hurried in. "I am sorry to interrupt, but you must come talk to Constance. She is most upset and will not stop crying."

Fiona turned to him. "I must go."

"Yes."

He started to leave as well.

"Lord Haversly?"

He turned back to her, a question in his eyes.

"I—Thank you for, well, for staying to speak to me. That is, I—well, I appreciate it."

A teardrop still lingered on the edge of one of her eyelashes. Her cheek was marked with the stain of a tear. She looked fragile and very lovely. William carried the echo of her halting words of gratitude out into the cool night air.

Fiona awoke the next morning feeling cheerless. The memory of last night came back in full force. She recalled the pleasant beginning to the evening, then the squabbling between the dowagers, and the final eruption between the two men. She tried not to think about the hour she had spent sitting in Constance's room listening to her sister cry inconsolably.

Pushing back the covers, Fiona got resolutely out of bed. She dressed without assistance in a flowing green gown and made her way downstairs to the breakfast room.

An atmosphere of mourning hung in the air. The maids who served breakfast talked in quiet whispers. When Mrs. Dyer appeared, she was reserved. She spoke only of the weather, but she did so in such sympathetic and sorrowful tones that Fiona was put in mind of a death or a funeral.

Several minutes later, Constance came downstairs walking with slow, listless steps.

The day continued, dragging with it a sense of doom.

No gentlemen callers presented themselves this morning. There were no flowers, no bits of verse written on stationery topped with crests. James Haversly did not call either. For this, at least, Fiona was grateful.

But the day was not destined to pass without some intercourse with the outside world. Women began to call after luncheon. Fiona had been expecting the gossip mongers.

Jessica Ormly oozed sympathy but clearly itched for more information. She hung at the edge of her chair pressing Fiona. "I do not mean to pry, dear, dear Fiona, but precisely how *did* Sir Geoffrey and Lord Lanton come to be seated near each other? Everyone knows that . . ." She paused delicately. "Well, everyone knows."

"It was an oversight," Fiona murmured while Constance sat beside her looking guilty and miserable. Fiona picked up a plate of shortbread and shoved it at the guest. "Jessica, *do* taste some of this shortbread. It is Cook's best. I am persuaded you will like it."

"But such an oversight!"

"The jams are also superb." She thrust strawberry jam at her guest.

Jessica was soon joined by Henrietta Small. Others followed.

Fiona was relentlessly polite as she endured the

visits and counted the minutes until each guest left. Constance sat stoically silent, although Fiona noticed her looking at the clock above the mantel from time to time.

Once the last guest had taken her leave, Fiona turned to her sister. "You see how it is, dear. I fear the chance of your making a good match this Season is dim." Fiona was acutely mindful of the fact Lord Borough, the man on whom she had pinned her fondest hope, had not called this morning.

Gently, she continued, "I suspect this will only be a nine days wonder. Next Season, when it is no longer the talk of the town, you can make a fresh start."

Constance sat staring at her hands in silence. "I do not want to leave London."

Fiona was dismayed. Did her sister still believe she could stay and enjoy the Season the way she had before? That would most assuredly not be the case. Their names would be slashed from guest lists all over London. Not everyone would abandon them, of course, but enough people would that it would make a difference.

Gently, Fiona leaned forward and touched her sister's hand. "You must be sensible. Things will not be as they have been. You will no longer be so sought after as a dance partner. We will be excluded from parties. That is the way of society. You must believe that it is the wisest course for us to go back to Surrey and let this whole affair fade away."

Constance rose, walked to the window and stared quietly out at a pair of doves on the lawn.

"Do you agree?" Fiona prompted.

"Have I a choice?" her sister asked after a long silence.

"No dear. We must return home."

"Then that is how it must be." Constance turned toward her. "Mama will be most disappointed."

"Mama will understand." In her heart, though, Fiona hated to carry bad news back to her mother. Mama had enough burdens worrying about Grove living in the wilds of the Cornish moors with neither wife nor family. But Mama would cope.

Constance left the room a few moments later and returned to her room. Fiona did not see her the rest of the day. That evening at dinner she spoke only when addressed, and she scarcely touched her food.

She was still subdued the next morning. When a maid appeared at breakfast with a note from James Haversly, Fiona did not even object. If he had written anything that could cheer Constance, Fiona would be glad of it.

As far as writing, she had her own to attend to. She had promised Mama she would convey all the details of Constance's party as soon as it was over. Fiona could procrastinate no longer. Besides, she must let her mother know she and Constance would be coming home.

With heavy heart, Fiona sat down at her desk and tried to think of some way to begin the letter.

She had still not written the first word when Mrs. Dyer rushed into the room. Her cheeks were crimson and her bosom heaved. "She is gone!"

"Who is gone?"

"Constance."

"No, she is in her room," Fiona said. "I saw her not an hour ago at breakfast."

"She is not there. She left this."

Fiona looked at the envelope Mrs. Dyer waved and swallowed a lump of misgiving.

"It was on her pillow. Her maid just found it." Mrs. Dyer thrust it at Fiona.

Fiona used the edge of her pen to slice the letter open. She drew in a fortifying breath and read.

Dear Sister,

James and I have decided we must act before we are separated. We have gone to Cornwall to beg Grove for his blessing. He is the one upon whom the quarrel rests between our families. If he will recognize what a wonderful person James is—and I am certain that he will—then everything will be all right. Please do not worry. I know what I am about.

Yours, etc.
Constance.

Fiona laid the note on the table and stared at it as if it were a thing alive. "Dear heavens," she whispered thickly.

Mrs. Dyer wrung her hands. "Never say that she has run off to Gretna Green."

"Worse. She has gone to Cornwall with James Haversly."

"Oh, no." The chaperone closed her eyes. "I fear I need smelling salts."

Fiona's mind worked feverishly. Her sister could not have been gone above an hour. There was still time to overtake them with a set of fast horses. No one knew of Constance's flight except Fiona and Mrs. Dyer. If they could keep word from getting about, Constance's reputation might yet be saved. Fiona's mind raced. What of their absence? After the embarrassment of the party, she reasoned, no one would be surprised if Constance or Fiona did not appear in public for a few days.

If Fiona caught up with Constance, scandal might yet be averted. Constance would not be the first girl to make a foolish mistake, but with luck this mistake could be hidden.

"We must go after her," Fiona directed. Moving briskly toward the door, she continued, "See to having your things packed. I shall order the carriage put to at once."

"We are going to try to stop them?"

"Yes."

The next two hours passed in a whirlwind. Fiona told the startled servants that Grove was ill and Constance had been sent with a friend to see him. Fiona herself, she explained, had tarried only long enough to make parting arrangements.

Then she rushed upstairs and helped her maid with the packing. She recklessly threw in delicate undergarments and walking dresses without regard for how they were folded.

Once everything had been put into two bandboxes, she sat at the door and waited for the carriage. And she fretted. She had no idea what sort of vehicle James Haversly drove, but she suspected it was something sleek and fast. Could she and Mrs. Dyer overtake him in their lumbering carriage? Alas, she had nothing smaller that would serve for a long trip. She must trust that the righteousness of their cause would give them speed.

Finally, the carriage was brought to the front of the house. In the confusion of bandboxes and neighing horses, Fiona did not wait to be helped into the carriage. She climbed in beside Mrs. Dyer, touched nervously at her bonnet, and signaled the driver to leave. She heard him give a sharp command to the horses. The carriage started forward.

It was not long before they left their own wide street of redbrick houses behind and headed into a tangle of narrow streets.

Mrs. Dyer looked out the window with a worried expression. "Dear me, we are going at quite a clip."

"I sent word to the driver to make haste," Fiona said from her corner of the carriage. He was going faster than she had expected, but she did not wish to slow him down. At this speed, they might catch Constance before the day was out. If only they could.

Suddenly, an unwelcome doubt crossed her mind. Fiona was not certain what she would do once she had Constance in hand. Fiona disliked the thought of taking her sister back to Surrey by force. But what if Constance refused to leave James?

There was also the matter of Grove. If the young people did make it to Cornwall, how would he react to seeing Constance with the brother—and veritable image—of the man who had shot him? Fiona plucked anxiously at her bonnet strings. It was all a terrible coil. If only Constance had not fallen prey to this unfortunate attraction to James Haversly.

Two hours passed. They left the winding, crowded streets of London behind and headed out the straight open road going west. The driver continued at a fast pace. Once he clipped a wheel into a ditch, and Fiona thought the whole carriage was going to go over.

Mrs. Dyer looked at her in alarm. "Mr. Sanders is going to see us all in our graves."

Fiona sighed. He was driving too fast. As anxious as she was to catch up with Constance, it was not worth risking their lives to do so. Reaching up, she pulled the string. When he leaned back to see what she wanted, she directed him to slow down.

He obeyed, moderating the speed to a comfortable

trot. Mrs. Dyer breathed an audible sigh of relief.

Fiona sank back against the squabs and into her thoughts. If only James Haversly had not been in London the Season that Constance was presented. If only Fiona had not let William Haversly persuade her that James and Constance should see each other. If only . . .

Such pointless speculation. It was too late to change the past. All she could do was try to keep the situation from getting worse. She dearly wished to keep Grove from coming face-to-face with James. How could Constance have been so foolish as to think all this could be sorted out if James and Grove met? Some things were too badly broken to be fixed. The relations between the Haverslys and the Baileys were certainly beyond repair.

"We seem to have gained speed again," Mrs. Dyer complained.

Fiona looked up and was touched with alarm. They were indeed moving at a fast pace. So fast that the carriage swayed fiercely. Just then they rounded a sharp curve. A wheel slipped off into the ditch, and the carriage pitched to the side. Fiona slid helplessly toward one end of the seat. She saw Mrs. Dyer clutching wildly for support. Fiona saw the wall coming up to meet her. She screamed.

Chapter 10

*T*HE CARRIAGE landed with a sharp thud at an odd angle. Fiona sat dazed. Gingerly, she moved her arms. They felt sore. They were bruised, but nothing seemed broken.

Shaking, she looked to her companion. "Are you all right, Mrs. Dyer?"

The older woman took a deep breath. "Yes, I—I think so." With trembling fingers she adjusted the bonnet that had been knocked askew.

Fiona sat another moment trying to calm herself. Then she moved carefully to the window and looked out. She saw they were wedged up against a ditch at an awkward tilt. It took an effort, but she finally managed to wrench the door open and jump the three feet to the ground.

She stood unsteadily for a moment. Then she hiked her skirts up above her half boots and walked to the front of the carriage. Mr. Sanders still sat on the tilted perch of the driver's seat. He looked sheepishly down at her. The boy who had been riding with him stood on the ground, his face white.

"We shall have it out in no time." Mr. Sanders gestured toward the boy. "I'll send Tom to the nearest town for help."

Fiona looked closely at the driver and saw what

she had been too flustered and preoccupied to see before they left London. His eyes were red and bleary.

"Mr. Sanders, were you drinking last night?" she asked.

He looked away. "No."

She stared at him. "Must I repeat the question?"

"Well, I may have had one or two drinks," he allowed. "Not more than three."

"No doubt you were still feeling the effects of them today."

"No, ma'am, I—"

Furious, she turned on her heel and marched away. Mrs. Dyer had somehow managed to climb out and stood beside the door ruefully examining a rip in her sleeve. "What happened?" she asked.

"Mr. Sanders was drinking last night," she announced angrily. "I daresay he was still half-foxed today." The fact she was still suffering from the lingering effects of her fright made the pitch of her anger higher.

Mrs. Dyer was indignant. "The wretch! We could have been killed."

Fiona looked over to see the boy unhitching the skittish horses. Even if Tom got help, what was Fiona to do once the carriage was out of the ditch and righted? She had no wish to jeopardize her life further. On the other hand, she could not give up her mission to reach Constance.

"We must send the boy back to London to hire a coach," Mrs. Dyer said with resolve.

Fiona hesitated. As upset as she was with Mr. Sanders, he was the only driver they had. "We are miles from London. We would lose an enormous amount of time if Tom went all the way back there.

It would take even more time for someone to get back here." Time was something Fiona did not have to lose.

Mrs. Dyer looked at her. "Surely you cannot mean to continue on with this man." She looked toward the chastened Mr. Sanders as if he were a troll.

"The accident has jolted him into soberness," Fiona temporized. "Tom can go somewhere nearby and get two or three strong men to help lift the carriage out of the ditch. Then we can be on our way." Was that the right decision?

Mrs. Dyer marched over to confront Mr. Sanders who now stood beside the toppled carriage. Glaring at him, she demanded, "What is the meaning of putting our lives in danger, sir?"

He shuffled his feet and looked at the pattern they made in the dust. "I had to go fast. Miss Bailey wished to arrive at her brother's house as soon as possible. He is ill, you know."

"She did not wish to arrive in Cornwall at the expense of our health."

Agitated, Fiona turned to watch Tom mount a horse and ride off. Mrs. Dyer stamped across the road to a bank and sat on it, her back stiff with anger. Fiona looked away. What a terrible coil. And with every minute that passed, Constance and James were getting further and further away.

As she stood helplessly by the wrecked carriage, a pony cart drove by. The two elderly occupants looked out curiously, then stopped. But they could do no more than offer a few words of sympathy. Not long after they left, the mail coach sped past. It moved by the wreckage with the same speed and abandon with which it passed every accident. Mail coach drivers were not trained to be helpful to fellow travelers.

They were trained to be fast and to deliver the mail as quickly as possible.

Fiona stood fretfully, blinking occasionally to hold back the tears of self-pity and frustration. She looked up again when she heard another vehicle approaching. It rounded the corner amid a blaze of blue and a showing of gold crest.

What in the world? It was Lord Haversly's carriage.

The startled driver pulled back on the reins. Several hundred feet down the road, the carriage came to a full stop. The door opened, and Lord Haversly stepped out. He surveyed the scene in a quick glance, then walked up to her.

"What happened?" he demanded.

"We had an accident. We have sent for help." She blinked furiously and tried to look as if she had the situation well under control. It didn't work. He frowned, as if he heard the underlying anxiety in her voice.

"Are you hurt?" he asked.

She rubbed at her arms. They felt tender where she had slammed hard into the wall of the carriage. "I am sore but not injured."

"You are going after your sister," he said. It was a flat statement, not a question.

"How did you know?" she asked. Was the news out over London?

"I had a note from my brother."

"Oh." Fiona was relieved. After a moment, she added honestly, "I must own it surprises me that you would try to stop them. I am gratified. If both you and I try to prevent an impetuous marriage, they may be made to see reason."

"It was not my intent to stop them from marrying," he said crisply.

"Then why are you going after them?"

"Out of concern for my brother's safety. I intend to make certain Grove does not do him any injury. Grove has been known to take unfair advantage before."

Fiona stared in disbelief. "*You* are the one who took unfair advantage before," she finally managed to sputter. She lifted her head. "That you would say such terrible things to me when I am alone on the road with a disabled carriage is the outside of enough." She wanted to be crushing, but the words came out sounding anguished.

He looked down at her. Some of the flintiness left his eyes, and his expression softened. "This is not the place for arguments. Let me examine the carriage." He turned and went to look at the carriage. Then he spent a few moments talking to the driver.

When he returned to her his face was harsh again. "Damnit, Fiona, what possessed you to get into a carriage with that man at the reins? Could you not see he has been drinking?"

"Well, I—"

"You are fortunate you were not killed." He glared down at her.

Fiona had had enough of bad luck and angry people this morning. "It would have been my own concern if I had been killed," she snapped. It was wretched enough that she was in this predicament; she did not need him or anyone else scolding her.

"You have made it my concern and that of any person who travels this road. By allowing a drunkard to manage your reins you have endangered us all." The gray eyes were fierce with accusation.

She looked wordlessly up at him. She could see that his emotions were on edge. For a moment, Fiona wondered if that was because he had been frightened to see her carriage wrecked. But no, that would imply a concern for her he did not possess.

She took a deep breath and forced herself to be calm. "Lord Haversly, I do not wish to stand here and be shouted at. Since my carriage will soon be righted, and I shall be on my way again, there is no further need for you to remain."

"Do you think I would go off and leave a lady stranded beside the road?" He looked around as if a thought had just occurred to him. "Are you alone?" he asked incredulously.

"No, Mrs. Dyer is with me." She gestured vaguely across to the chaperone, who took that as a sign to join them and immediately scrambled to her feet.

"Even when the carriage is ready to go again," he continued, "you cannot ride with that man. You have no way to prevent him from getting drunk again tonight. The only sensible course is for you to ride in my carriage. We are, after all, both bound for the same place."

Mrs. Dyer appeared at Fiona's side. "That is an eminently sensible suggestion. We should either go with the earl or return to London."

"We cannot go back," Fiona said. Her mind made up, she added firmly, "And we will not travel with Lord Haversly."

Mrs. Dyer's mouth pared into a thin line. "I daresay *his* driver is sober. I certainly have no wish to risk my life again in the hands of Mr. Sanders. Once the boy returns with help, he and Mr. Sanders can take the carriage back to London."

Fiona stood mutely. Her nerves were stretched tautly all the way around. Not for the first time today, she wished she had someone to take over her cares. But there was no one. "I will not ride in Lord Haversly's carriage," she repeated.

"Fiona, forget your pride and listen to reason for once," William said bluntly. "If you are afraid I will join you in the carriage, you need not fear. I will ride a horse, and you can have the carriage to yourself."

Fiona knew if she did not accept Lord Haversly's offer, she would have to contend with an angry Mrs. Dyer the rest of the trip. Even worse was the worry that she could not depend on Mr. Sanders staying sober. She was trapped. The idea of going in Lord Haversly's carriage rankled her, but there was no good alternative.

"Why do we stand here wasting time?" William demanded with an impatient snap of his gloves against his palm. "Isn't the important thing to catch up with Constance and James?"

Yes, Fiona acknowledged silently. That *was* what mattered. Except for a blow to her pride, did it matter which carriage they were in when they overtook the young couple?

As long as William was not riding with her and Mrs. Dyer, it would be bearable, she reasoned with herself. Besides, William Haversly owed her the use of his carriage since he was the one who had convinced her to let the two young people see each other. *This* was what had come of it.

"Very well, I accept," she said without inflection.

Out of the corner of her eye, she caught Mrs. Dyer's nod of approval.

Fiona turned to William. "Thank you for your offer." The words stuck in her throat, but she forced them out. She hated to admit it, but she felt more at ease now that William was part of the expedition. It solved a lot of problems to be with a man of rank. How she would feel once they reached Grove's house was something she did not want to consider.

William set a comfortable pace on his roan horse. If he were to ride hard, he might overtake the young lovers and that would please Fiona. His concern, however, was not with preventing an elopement but with keeping Grove from doing anything rash once James and Grove met.

At any rate, William was not going to wear himself out riding hard on the first day. Cornwall was a long way from London, and he had not thought he would be spending most of it in the saddle. He was doing so only because he had told Fiona he would.

If he rode in the carriage he suspected he would have to suffer tense silence. He was sure Fiona blamed him for the way events had turned out. He would never convince her that matters had probably been headed this way whether or not she gave her approval for James to call on Constance.

Still, he felt sorry for her. It had been a shock to round the corner in his carriage and see a forlorn-looking Fiona standing beside a wrecked coach. She should never have been in the position of having to go after Constance. That should have been Grove's responsibility. William wondered if Fiona would ever accept the fact that her brother was a black-guard unworthy of her loyalty.

*   *   *

William Haversly's carriage was well appointed and the squabs comfortable, Fiona had to admit. Still, it was a long ride, and her back was beginning to ache by the time they finally stopped for the night at an inn.

Lord Haversly was standing at the carriage door when it opened.

"Did you catch up with Constance and James?" she demanded anxiously.

"No."

"Oh." She didn't try to hide her disappointment. Evening was falling, and that changed the nature of things considerably. As long as Constance and James were out alone in the daytime, their reputations might be salvaged, but if they spent a night alone, her sister would be ruined.

William offered his hand. His touch seemed gentle, and she sensed that he meant to be consoling. When she looked up at him, he smiled. She nodded and looked back down.

He assisted Mrs. Dyer in alighting, then motioned toward the inn. "I am afraid it does not offer much. They only have two rooms with parlors. I have engaged them both. There is, however, ample room for the servants."

Fiona understood his meaningful look toward Mrs. Dyer. That good lady was not a servant and could not be expected to stay in the common servants' quarters. Since Lord Haversly would take one of the rooms with parlors, that meant Mrs. Dyer and Fiona would have to share a room.

Fiona had hoped to have some time alone, but clearly it was not to be. She bit back further disappointment.

"I am sorry," Lord Haversly said in an undertone to Fiona as they started toward the mortar and daub building.

"It is not your fault."

"I am exhausted," Mrs. Dyer said from behind them. "I hope we can be shown our rooms soon."

"Yes, of course," Lord Haversly said.

Inside, a girl with a long braid showed Fiona and the chaperone up the steps to a long, multi-windowed room. It was simple but clean. The two blue chairs by the fireplace looked comfortable. A fire blazing in the grate took the chill off the evening.

Fiona removed her sage green bonnet and shook out her curls. She longed for the luxury of a bath but knew that would take too long to prepare. Instead, she stretched her tired limbs and sat in one of the chairs.

A short time later a cold supper was sent up. After they ate, Mrs. Dyer rose stiffly.

"I do not wish to be unsocial, but I shall collapse if I do not go to bed now."

"It has been a long day," Fiona agreed. Even though her body was weary, her thoughts raced, and she knew it would be hopeless for her to try to sleep. Worries about Constance and about how Grove would react when he learned his sister wanted to marry James Haversly kept her from relaxing.

She fidgeted in the chair while Mrs. Dyer went about the business of preparing for bed. Perhaps a walk in the little herb garden that she had noticed behind the building would calm her, Fiona thought.

Rising, she pulled a wrap over her shoulders and went down the steps and out the back door of the inn. Pausing outside the door, she pulled the shawl tighter. A full moon bathed the garden in light. Ordinarily, she would have marveled at the beauty of the evening. Tonight, she was too unhappy to give it more than passing notice.

The fragrance of lavender scented the night air. It was a perfect summer night, and she and Constance should be enjoying it back in London.

As she walked amid the plants, she fingered the loose fringe on her shawl. In the silence of the garden, she could think clearly for the first time all day. She finally admitted what she had been trying to deny all day: it was futile to try to stop what had already been set in motion. Constance and James had run away together. She was deceiving herself if she thought she could keep word of that from getting out. Her sister had been in a carriage all day with the man. Fiona could not bear to think where or under what circumstances they might be spending the night.

It pained her, but there was no other choice now except for them to marry.

As she rounded a corner, a distinctly unherbal scent hit her. She looked down the path and saw the red tip of a cheroot. Even in the uncertain light, she could make out the well-proportioned form of Lord Haversly.

"Good evening, Fiona," he said quietly.

"Good evening."

She remained where she stood by the rosemary. William continued to stand at the end of the path a few yards away. Neither spoke.

After a time, the silence grew uncomfortable. "Thank you for the use of your carriage today," she said.

"You are welcome."

"It was most unfortunate what happened with our coachman."

"Yes."

She was mute again. Then, she said what was uppermost in her mind, "There is nothing for it now but for James to marry Constance. I hope you will support me in that decision."

"I will."

"There will be a scandal, of course," she worried aloud. "People are bound to talk about the unseemliness of it all."

"People always talk." His short laugh held no humor. "Your family and mine are no strangers to scandal, Fiona, especially when it concerns each other."

"No." He moved a few steps closer, stopping by the holly.

Silence was upon them again, and she cast about for something to say. "Why were you out here in the dark?"

"To be honest, I am worried about seeing Grove after all these years."

What a strange thing to say. She had never thought William had any sensitivity at all toward Grove. Or was he afraid? "Do you think he will challenge you to a duel?"

William's laugh was cynical. "If he did, I would not accept. I am not a foolish young cawker any longer."

"I don't know what you mean." She pulled at the fringe on her shawl.

"I have responsibilities now and people in London who need me. People all over England need me. I would not be so stupid as to stand in the way of a gun again."

She sank down on a bench and looked up at him. The moonlight shadowed his face so that he looked like a stranger to her. "Are you talking about the children in factories?" she asked.

"Yes."

"Why did you decide to champion their cause?" She wanted him to continue talking. It soothed her to listen, and it diverted her for a moment from thoughts of her problems.

He sat down beside her and clasped his hands in front of him. "When I was in Spain I saw a great deal of poverty. That was just after the duel."

"Yes, I know." She did not want to dwell on that. "Go on."

"I told everyone how shocking it was to see children living in such conditions. Finally, someone told me I should go back to my own country and look at how many of our own children lived." He paused, then continued slowly, "I did, and I was ashamed. At first I waited for others to do something. When I realized the condition of those children mattered little to men with money and property, I decided I must be the one to act."

Fiona looked at the man beside her. He had done a horrible thing to her brother. But in the years since, he had worked tirelessly on behalf of those children. Had that been his way of atoning for what he had done to Grove? William had changed in the years since the duel. Could she still hold him responsible for what a younger, more impetuous William had done in the heat of jealousy? Part of her still did. But part of her was no longer so sure.

Maybe for Grove and William to come face-to-face at last would resolve something for everyone. If Grove could see that William had changed and could forgive him, perhaps she could, too.

William's thoughts must have been following a similar track, for he said carefully, "Fiona, if Constance and James marry, our families cannot continue to be at dagger's drawing."

"No." The smell of the cheroot still hung with him, and she found she liked the scent.

"Even if Grove does not accept the match, you and I must make an effort to bring the families together. After all, there will probably be children, and you would not want to be estranged from your nephews and nieces."

"No, I would not." She found it difficult to imagine Constance with children. But that, of course, was what would happen. She knew she could not cut herself off from Constance's children; it would pain her far too much.

"Fiona, do you think you and I could be friends—for the sake of James and Constance?"

"I am willing to try," she said softly.

"And to forget about the past?"

She hesitated on that. The duel was such a large thing to forget. But in the years since, William Haversly had become a man of honor even if he had been without honor at the time.

"Yes, to forget the past," she murmured and looked up at him. He was looking steadily down at her, but for once that did not make her uneasy. In fact, she felt comfortable sitting beside him and enjoying the newfound truce. They remained together for several more minutes watching the moonlight glimmer in the garden and smelling the lavender.

At length she rose to go in. They exchanged simple good-nights and she went back to her room feeling calmer than she had felt in some time.

Chapter 11

*T*HE PARTY left at daybreak the next morning. Mrs. Dyer and Fiona settled into the carriage, and William rode away on his horse. By nine, they had already made some distance.

The long hours in the carriage slowly began to tell on Fiona. And on Mrs. Dyer. By midmorning, Mrs. Dyer's constant twitching of her rings was annoying Fiona.

They were near Basingstoke, when the chaperone said, "I do believe the dust would not be so bad in here if you would close your window more securely."

"It is closed, Mrs. Dyer."

"Are you certain? I can see cracks around it and I can positively *feel* the dust seeping in. Perhaps you could put your handkerchief over the window."

"That would block my light."

"Darkness is preferable to all this dust."

Fiona chose to ignore that. A short time after, Mrs. Dyer fell asleep and began to wheeze through her nose. Biting her tongue, Fiona looked out the window.

She was thankful when they stopped for tea at an inn.

Lord Haversly was already there, coated with road

dust but looking invigorated from the hours in the saddle.

"The air seems to agree with you," she said as he held the door for her and she followed Mrs. Dyer inside and up the stairs to a private parlor.

"Is the carriage comfortable?" he asked politely.

"Very, but it grows tiresome."

"Then you should take a mount and ride with me."

She made no reply as a maid bustled through with a tray of bisquits. Ladies rode in covered vehicles, protected from the wind and sun and out of sight of the common people who traveled the roads. It would be unseemly for her to ride.

When they left the inn, however, her gaze drifted longingly toward the earl's saddled steed.

He saw the direction of her look. "Are you sure you would not like to join me? It would only take a moment to unhitch one of the extra horses and saddle it."

"I do not mean to cause any trouble," she demurred, her gaze still resting longingly on his mount.

He laughed. "You say that without conviction." He turned to address the groom, "Prepare the dappled one for a rider."

Within five minutes Fiona was seated on a dappled gray. Since she was not wearing a riding skirt, it took a few minutes to arrange the folds of her rose-colored skirts appropriately. Lord Haversly waited patiently as the carriage rolled out ahead of them.

Fiona was not sorry to see it go. "The ride *had* become tedious," she confided as she tied the ribbons around her bonnet tighter in preparation of the ride.

"I suspected as much."

Although she had ridden along Rotten Row in London a number of times in the past weeks, it had always been at a maddeningly sedate pace. This horse, with its prancing step and tossing mane, seemed very capable of giving her a good ride.

"I am ready," she announced and urged the horse forward. It responded to her signals as if it had been carrying her on its back all its life. Fiona lifted her face and let the wind graze the sides of her cheeks.

William was slightly ahead of her. He looked back. "Am I going too fast?"

She smiled. "Never."

"There was a time you could not match my pace." His tone was comfortable and teasing.

She tossed her head. "I assure you you are quite wrong, sir. I was always capable of holding my own, even with you."

He fell back beside her. "That sounds remarkably like a challenge."

She saw the glint of competition in his eyes and an answering spirit of competition rose up inside her. "The question of who is the better rider could be settled easily enough."

"I daresay it could." Already his fingers tightened on the reins in anticipation.

"We could race." They had not passed anyone other than donkey carts for the past two hours. What harm could there be in indulging in the urge to let herself go?

"Done," he replied.

They were off before she had a chance to do more than look down the road. Her horse was fleet and sure, and the road was smoothly worn. Her bonnet was soon blown back and her hair tangled by the wind. They passed the carriage and soon left it behind. She spared only a moment to wonder what Mrs. Dyer would say if she looked out and saw Fiona racing down the road. Then she forgot the question altogether and delighted in the freedom of the moment.

She was aware of hooves flying beside her as she leaned close to the horse's neck. William was giving her a good run. The last time she could remember giving a horse its head in this manner was in the old days when she and William and Grove and Eliza had challenged one another. She had forgotten how exhilarating it could feel. She would have been content to pummel down the road like this all day.

But a short time later she rounded a curve and saw that the road ended not far away where a broad river crossed it. The only way across the river was by ferry.

Reluctantly she pulled her horse to a halt. Beside her, William did the same.

She shook back her hair and turned to him with a smile.

He slid off his horse and came over to her side. She gave him her hand and slipped to the ground beside him.

"The ferry is gone. We shall have to wait," he said.

"Yes." She was still breathless and excited.

He led the way to a tree beside the river. They sat down and looked out at the river. The sun reflecting off the water shimmered golden.

Fiona leaned back against the trunk and closed her eyes. "That felt wonderful. I have not ridden so hard for years."

"Nor I. I am so seldom out of London."

She opened her eyes and looked at him. "I daresay you cannot afford to be away from Parliament long."

"I cannot. This is a particularly bad time to be

gone. An important vote is coming up, and I must be there." He paused, then asked, "What about you? Will you go back to London?"

"No. There is no need to. I was only there to present Constance." Ruefully, she added, "I certainly failed in that job."

"Not if she is happy."

The breeze ruffled her hair, and she pushed her fingers through it restlessly. "A woman's choices cannot be based entirely on feelings. There are other matters to consider, like her position and her family's financial situation."

He turned to her. "If you believe so strongly in marriage as a business proposition, then why did you never marry, Fiona?"

His gaze was too intent, and his question cut too close to the bone. She looked away. "I never found the right person."

"Do you mean you never found a man with the right connections and social standing, or you never found a man you loved?"

The question was impertinent. "I do not wish to discuss the matter," she said haughtily. Talk of love made her feel self-conscious and confused. She looked toward the road. "What can be taking the carriage so long? And where is the ferry?"

"They will be here in due time. We will be in Cornwall soon enough," he added. "How long has it been since you last visited your brother?"

"I have never been to visit Grove." At his look of surprise, she added quickly, "There was never a convenient time for me to go." Once or twice she had planned a trip, but it had never been a good time for Grove, and he had written to her asking her to postpone her trip.

"I see."

"He is very busy," she added.

"You do not need to apologize for him."

"I am not apologizing." She smoothed her dress with restless fingers, then admitted with a sigh, "Perhaps I am. Grove is no longer so interested in his family as we would like."

"How do you think he will receive Constance?" William asked bluntly.

"I am more concerned with how he will receive *you*. I cannot think he will be glad to see you." The few times William's name had come up between Fiona and her brother, Grove had still been bitter.

She laid her hand impulsively atop William's. "If you were to apologize to Grove for what happened and tell him you acted out of the foolishness and arrogance of youth, he might forgive you. The two of you might be able to rebuild the friendship you once had."

William withdrew his hand. "You mistake the matter, Fiona, and you always have. If anyone is to beg pardon, it is Grove."

"But you shot him without warning. Do not look at me like that. I do not want to argue with you. I want to help heal the breach between you." It was the first time she had felt a desire to do so.

"I did not shoot without warning. That is what you prefer to believe and what your father insisted on believing. That is not what happened," he said coldly.

"You fled the country," she pointed out, trying to hold on to her patience.

"Out of stupidity, not because I did anything wrong." He stared hard at her, as if trying to impart something to her by the force of his gaze. "Wrong was done, but it was *to* me and not *by* me."

"Are you accusing Grove?" She felt a sinking sense of helplessness. Until William would admit and apologize for what he had done, nothing could be settled.

"Fiona, everything Grove told you was a lie. I may not be a saint, but I am not a criminal. Shooting me was not even the worst of his crimes. He held up carriages at gunpoint in the middle of the night."

She shook her head. "I don't understand what you are saying." Was William's guilt over what he did to her brother so fierce that he must manufacture the worst possible lies in order to justify himself? What had this story about holding up a man on the highway to do with anything?

"I am saying you do not know the man you have believed in so strongly all these years. Neither have you been well repaid for your loyalty. I doubt Grove has any brotherly feelings at all for you or for Constance."

He rose, and she scrambled to her feet after him. The carriage came into view, but she ignored it. "Why do you hate Grove so much?" she demanded passionately. "Was it because he stole a woman away all those years ago? Surely that cannot be the whole reason."

He grabbed at her wrists. "Fiona, there was no woman. If anything, I was in love with you at the time. But your brother involved me in highway robbery, and for that I called him out."

"He involved you in robbery," she repeated in confusion.

The carriage stopped nearby, and Mrs. Dyer alighted.

"Yes, for entertainment or because his pockets were to let or for some perverse reason only he would know, he held up a man and took his money and rings. I saw the whole thing."

Dazed, Fiona stared at him. Everyone had heard of highwaymen. They were ruthless and nasty and deserved to be hung. But Grove? It simply was not possible. And yet here stood William looking down at her with eyes that insisted she believe him.

Mrs. Dyer approached. She looked at the two tense people and asked delicately. "Is anything amiss?"

William dropped Fiona's hands and stepped away. "No, we are perfectly fine."

"I see the ferry coming." The older woman still watched them curiously.

Shaken and in a fog, Fiona boarded the ferry and watched the water rippling near her feet as the boat moved across the river. Her thoughts were in chaos. What William suggested about Grove was absolutely ludicrous. But he spoke with such fierce conviction it was difficult to dismiss everything he had said. If she were to believe him, though, that meant her brother was a scoundrel of the blackest kind.

Also vivid in her mind was the sentence sandwiched in the middle of all the other explanations and accusations. "If anything I was in love with you at the time."

Fiona was up early the next morning, dressed and waiting for the carriage to take her the remainder of the way to Cornwall and to her brother. She had passed a long and sleepless night with all manner of things going round in her head. She was worried about Constance and about Grove. She was also preoccupied with thoughts of Lord Haversly.

Yet she avoided seeing him before they left. When she did spy him briefly as he was mounting his horse, she looked away, confused by her tangled feelings from yesterday.

Mrs. Dyer made feeble attempts at conversation, and Fiona tried to respond. But she was distracted. The gnawing in the pit of her stomach grew ever more intense as they neared Cornwall. She wanted to see Grove, and at the same time she dreaded seeing him.

"The moors are very stark, are they not?" Mrs. Dyer said.

Although Fiona had been looking out the window, she had scarcely noticed the granite moors and the little fields divided by stone walls. "Yes," she said, "but pretty." Heather was scattered among the boulders and bog flora. In the distance she saw a small wood.

"So isolated, though," Mrs. Dyer continued. "It is difficult to conceive of anyone wishing to live all the way out here."

"Yes." Fiona had always thought Grove had chosen the isolation because his faith in human nature had been shattered, and he wished to be away from people. But if what William had said were true, then why had Grove really moved to this remote part of the kingdom?

It was near the end of the day, and shadows were lengthening before they finally turned down a lane. Fiona peered out the window and up the lane at a cobblestone manor house. Three years ago she had planned to come visit, but Grove had written that he was not well and asked her to wait until he was better. He had never written again to encourage her to make new plans.

At the time she had worried that Grove was short of funds and was too proud to apply to her or Mama for help. But her gently-worded letter offering assistance was never answered.

The carriage came to a halt in front of the house. William's efficient coachman opened the door and let down the steps. Fiona alighted and looked around.

It was not a large house, but it was well kept. Neatly trimmed little hedges surrounded the lower level. It did not appear that Grove wanted for money.

William walked up beside her, his boots crunching on the gravel. "I arrived just a few minutes ago. I have not yet tried the door. I wanted to wait until you arrived."

She nodded, walked up to the door, and lifted the door knocker. Her first thought was that it was a highly polished brass. Then she realized it was gold. "Good heavens," she murmured as she traced a finger over it.

"Very pretty," Mrs. Dyer said absently. "I hope we will be shown to rooms immediately. I am dreadfully tired."

The door opened and Fiona found herself looking at a footman in crimson attire and a white mustache. He bowed to her.

"I am here to see Grove Bailey. I am his sister," she said.

"The master is not home."

"When do you expect him?"

"I cannot say. Please do come in." He gestured her into the foyer.

"Fiona?" Constance's voice rang from the upper recesses of the house. Fiona looked up to see her sister gliding down a set of wide stairs, her traveling skirts billowing out behind her.

She reached out for her sister and engulfed her in a hug. "I have been so worried. Are you all right?"

"Yes. I am fine."

"Where is James Haversly?" Had he done something unspeakable to her sister? Had he abandoned Constance? All manner of unhappy thoughts ran through her mind.

Constance laughed and reassured her. "He has gone into town. We only arrived an hour ago. We took a wrong road and had to retrace our steps."

"Then you have not seen Grove?"

"No. I do not know where he is." Noticing William and Mrs. Dyer for the first time, she dropped a curtsey. "Good afternoon, Lord Haversly. I hope you are well, Mrs. Dyer?"

William ignored the pleasantries and demanded, "Why has my brother gone into town?"

"To find someone who can tell him where Grove may be. We need to find him right away." She colored, then continued, "We do not have a license. James thought Grove could help us get a special license so that we could be married right away. I hope you will not try to stop us, Fiona."

"I won't." She glanced toward the chaperone self-consciously. Now was not the time to have a discussion about marriage plans.

Mrs. Dyer had other thoughts on her mind. "Are there guest bedrooms?" she asked straightforwardly.

"Not many. I daresay Grove does not entertain out-of-town guests often. But the house is very nice," she added. "There is even a set of gold plates in the dining room."

"Really?" How odd to have such an extravagance. Then Fiona glanced around the foyer for the first time and took in the rich Oriental runner in the

153

hallway. The crystal drops on the chandelier gleamed like genuine Austrian crystal, and the landscape scene on the wall looked like a real Turner. Surely not, though, for such a painting would be very dear. She was sure Grove worked hard at managing his estate, but she doubted it produced enough income to allow him such luxuries.

Beside her, William also looked around. "Everything appears expensive," he noted.

"The picture is probably only a good imitation." She felt obliged to defend her brother even though no accusation had been made.

"Perhaps."

"If no one objects, I should like to go to a room," Mrs. Dyer said.

"I am sure that is fine." Fiona turned to the servant. "Please show my sister's chaperone to a guest room."

The footman led Mrs. Dyer up the steps. That left Fiona, Constance, and William alone in the foyer.

Constance looked at her. "I am sorry if I caused you any alarm, Fiona," she said guiltily. "I tried to make my note as soothing as possible."

"As long as you are all right, that is all that matters." There were questions of a more intimate nature Fiona wanted to ask, but she could not with William standing nearby.

He, however, had no such qualms about delicacy. "Where have you and James stayed these past nights?"

The younger woman blushed and looked down at her hands. "In an inn. In separate rooms," she added hastily.

Fiona colored. "Please, William, Constance and I can discuss all of this later. In private."

"I have to know now," he said tersely. "I must have the answers to any questions Grove asks."

He sounded as if he expected the worst when he came face-to-face with Grove, Fiona realized with a sense of foreboding.

"Why did James leave you here when he went into town?" William demanded of Constance.

"He wanted me to rest." She looked up at him with innocent, imploring eyes. "Please do not make things difficult for James. I am persuaded that everything can be settled once we explain our feelings for each other to Grove. My brother will come to love James."

William's expression softened. Fiona knew he held no such hope, but she was grateful to him for not destroying her sister's illusions.

William stepped back toward the door. "I am going into town to try to find James."

Fiona knew the correct thing would be to remain behind with Constance. But Mrs. Dyer was here, she told herself. "I will join you." She followed William out the door.

Fiona wanted to be present to try to temper the moment when William met Grove. Her sisterly feelings for Grove remained, although small doubts now marred them. A new need had been added: she must also make certain William was safe.

He stopped at his carriage and turned to her. "It is not necessary for you to go, Fiona. I would as lief you remain here."

"No. I am going."

"As you wish." He didn't smile at her, but she heard humor, even fondness in his words.

It took less than an hour for Fiona and William to reach the seaside town closest to Grove's house. The houses of the fishing village were stacked down the cliff that led to the water. The center of town was little more than a livery stable, a few shops, and an inn of white wood. The carriage stopped in the courtyard, and William went inside to make inquiries.

He returned several minutes later. She leaned forward anxiously but could read nothing in his face. "Well?" she demanded.

"James has been here, but the innkeeper did not know where he is now."

James was not the one Fiona was concerned about. "Did you ask about Grove?"

"Yes."

"What did they say?"

"That he is little seen around the village. Rumor has it he comes and goes frequently and is often away from home for days."

She brushed that aside with a shake of her head. "That is impossible. How could he manage an estate?"

"I asked that same question. The innkeeper said Grove does not own an estate. He owns only the house and a little bit of land around it."

She stared. "He could not support himself on a few meager acres. What would he live on?"

William made no reply.

The question hung between them. Fiona thought about the expensive-looking rugs, about the gold plates, and about the brother who seldom came to see the family. Resolutely, she pushed aside the seed of doubt. Her brother was not involved in illegal activities. It was simply not possible. Once Grove appeared, he would explain everything.

William turned to her with a troubled expression. But his touch was gentle as he took one of her hands in his and looked down at her with those deep gray eyes. "Fiona, it might be best if you and Constance returned home now, without seeing Grove. After all, Constance and James came here to get his approval for their marriage because they did not think you would give yours. But since you no longer oppose the match, it is not necessary to have Grove's blessing."

In the cozy interior of the carriage, with William holding her hand, Fiona was almost convinced.

"Your mother is certain to get word of the elopement," he continued. "The sooner you return to her and reassure her, the better." He spoke in low, reasonable tones. The whole time he kept looking at her with those persuasive gray eyes.

It was tempting to let him make the decisions. His shoulders looked strong and capable, and she had carried the burden for a long time. She shook herself, refusing to give in to the temptation. She had come a long way, and she could not leave without seeing her brother. "I must see Grove." She forced herself to continue, "If I have been wrong all these years, I need to learn that for myself. Besides," she added firmly, "I may not be wrong."

"I do not know whether to be annoyed with you or to admire you."

She withdrew her hand from his and tried to return the conversation to an impersonal level. "We should go back to the house. I do not wish to leave Constance by herself overlong." She was also thinking that Grove might return, and she wished to be there when Constance told him her news.

"Very well."

They started back in silence. Fiona sank to one side of the carriage, immersed in thought. If she was wrong about Grove, that changed everything she believed about William Haversly. He would not be a blackguard at all. He might even be a hero.

She thought about the work he did on behalf of factory children. Could a man put so much time and effort into such a selfless cause to atone for a past crime? Or was he doing it because he was a good man?

The drive back seemed to take a long time. Dusk fell, and it was necessary for the driver to go slower on the unfamiliar roads. Darkness had long fallen by the time they pulled up in front of the house. Another carriage arrived just after them, and a man got out of it. Fiona looked out and saw that the light from the house revealed him clearly. Grove. Fiona swallowed heavily. The moment of truth was near, and she was no longer sure she was ready for it.

Chapter 12

FIONA PEERED at her brother through the carriage and saw that he was dressed well but simply in a brown jacket and tan trousers. He looked tense as he surveyed their carriage. Did he recognize the crest? Fiona stepped out and saw a look of surprise lift the frown from his features.

"Hello, sister," Grove said.

She went to him, and he greeted her with a brief hug.

She hugged him back. He looked older. The lines on his face bespoke a toughness that must come from living out in this remote part of the country. It had been well over a year since she had seen him; his sandy hair was now peppered with gray.

He looked back toward the carriage and said, "That is not yours."

"No."

Fiona threw a glance over her shoulder. The earl must have decided to give them some time alone together before making his appearance. She turned back to her brother. "Could we go inside and talk?" she asked. "I have much to explain to you."

His gaze remained fixed on the carriage. "It is Haversly's," he said with slow deliberation.

She colored. "Yes, it is Lord Haversly's carriage. I

have come—that is, we both came because Constance fled here with the man she wishes to marry. He is William's younger brother, James."

"James? The young pup born when we were children?"

"Yes."

"He and Constance have run away together?"

"Yes." She waited for a reaction but saw none. He kept a steely gaze focused on the door of the carriage. Without looking at her, he asked, "Why did they come here?"

"Constance hoped you would give them your blessing." Fiona waited for a sign of any emotion. But he only remained aloof and cold as he idly kicked one booted foot against the ground. He seemed far more interested in the carriage than in his sister. Grove raised his voice. "If Haversly is in the carriage, why doesn't he get out?" He was not speaking to her but to the person in the carriage.

Fiona turned toward the grand vehicle. William heard the challenge and alighted.

Fiona saw the cold defiance on William's face. She looked at Grove. His impassive expression was even more frightening than raw anger would have been.

"What are you doing here, Will?" It might have been a pleasant question had there not been a knife edge to Grove's voice.

"I have come to assure myself you do not harm my brother."

Fiona watched. The two men did not take their eyes from each other; they looked like feral animals awaiting an attack if they blinked. Both men seemed to have completely forgotten her.

She started forward. "Grove, I came in Lord Haversly's carriage after my own met with an accident.

I know it must pain you to see him, but I am indebted to him."

"Where are you staying?" Grove asked her.

The question took Fiona aback. "I had thought we would stay with you." Constance and Mrs. Dyer had already had their baggage taken in.

"I see."

They were not welcome, Fiona realized, and the thought numbed her.

Just then the front door opened and her younger sister bounded out the door. Fiona felt a stab of pity as she watched Constance run to Grove. Her face was full of such innocence and hope that Fiona could not bear to look.

She turned away and met William's gaze. Wordlessly, he came over to her side.

"Has Fiona told you?" Constance demanded of Grove. "Has she told you I wish to wed James Haversly?"

"Yes."

"I am so anxious for you to meet him. He should be back soon. He has been gone some time now." She cast a worried look out toward the dark moors. "I do not like him being out on the roads after dark."

Fiona found the comfort in William's presence that she had not found in Grove's. However callous her brother had grown over the years, she thought he could at least feign happiness at seeing them. If not for her sake, then for Constance's. But he seemed distracted. He kept looking out into the darkness.

"Is everything all right, Grove?" she asked.

"Yes, what could be wrong?" he shot back tersely. Pivoting, he commanded, "Let us go inside."

William stood uncertainly. "You can come, too," Grove said shortly. "I may not like you, but I am too mindful of my sisters' presence to do you an injury."

On that gracious note, they went inside. Grove made no offer of food or other refreshment. He simply shouted for the servant that they had met upon their arrival. "Giles, find rooms for our guests."

Fiona moved over to stand beside her sister and put a reassuring hand on her shoulder. Constance stood silently in the hall and watched Grove.

"Do you not even want to hear about James?" she finally asked in a small voice.

He laughed. "I am persuaded you find him a top of the trees fellow."

"Yes, but I want you to like him, too. I do not understand why he has not returned by now." She cast another troubled look outside into the dark. "He does not know the moors. Do you think he could have gotten lost?"

That question seemed to catch Grove's interest. "Perhaps. I shall go look for him once you are settled. I know these roads well."

"Thank you," Constance said in relief.

Fiona reserved her gratitude. She sensed Grove was using the opportunity to escape. Did he want to leave simply because they were here? Still, she reminded herself, William was with them, and that was bound to color Grove's attitude.

Fiona and Constance followed the servant up the stairs. They were shown rooms on opposite sides of the hall. Fiona took only a moment to look at her room and to note that her baggage had already been deposited there. Then she went back downstairs again. She did not like the idea of leaving William and Grove alone.

In the foyer, she found the two men standing in tense silence.

"I am going to look for James," Grove told her. He ignored William.

"I will join you," William said.

"I do not need your assistance," he snapped.

Fiona had had enough. "Grove, we cannot continue like this. Things have changed. Yes, there was a duel, but it was a long time ago. Your sister wishes to marry a Haversly. We must try to make the best of that."

"Constance may do as she likes, but that does not mean I will have any love for William or his brother." Grove turned and stalked toward the door.

William was right behind him. Fiona stood frozen, uncertain what to do. It was not safe to let them go out into the darkness together. But how could she stop them?

Just then she heard the sound of a carriage drawing up. Both men stopped in their tracks.

"That must be James," she said.

"Yes," William said.

The door burst open, and a disheveled James burst in. He looked around in agitation before his gaze settled on his brother. "William, what are you doing here?"

"I came—"

Already the younger man's thoughts had jumped elsewhere. He swung toward Fiona. "Where is Constance? Is she all right?"

"Yes, of course. Why would she not be?"

"It isn't safe here. I was set upon by a highwayman as I crossed the moors. Robbed me of everything I had with me."

"Were you hurt?" Fiona asked quickly.

"No, but he carried a pistol, and he looked capable of using it."

"Then you saw his face?" William asked.

"No. It was dark. I could describe little about him." James noticed Grove for the first time.

Fiona stepped forward. "Grove, this is the Honorable James Haversly. He is the young man who desires to marry Constance. My brother, Grove Bailey."

Grove nodded. Fiona felt a flash of impatience with her brother. The least he could do was utter a few civil words.

"I am pleased to meet you," James said. "I hope you will forgive our impertinence in coming. But we were at wit's end, and we hoped for your approval." He paused uncertainly.

Grove nodded again. It was then Fiona realized that he deliberately was not speaking. How curious. She looked toward William and saw that he watched Grove keenly. An uneasy feeling swept over her, and she tried to brush it away. Something was wrong. She sensed other people in the room knew it, too. But she did not want to confront it.

"Why do we not have something to drink?" she suggested with a desperate brightness.

William shook his head. "No. I want to hear Grove say something to my brother. Anything. Why don't you say, 'Stand and deliver,' Grove?"

Everything happened at once.

She saw her brother move toward the door, saw the look of astonishment on James's face, and saw the lightning swiftness with which William tackled Grove.

In a blur of boots and breeches, she saw the two men go down. She saw the flash of a knife, heard someone running from somewhere in the house, and felt her own knuckles pressed tightly against her mouth.

Fiona would never after be able to reconstruct exactly what happened. She only knew there was a violent struggle and both men came up bleeding. Then James was in the midst of it and he, too, was cut and bleeding. Constance ran down the steps and hovered on the sidelines screaming.

Grove's servant materialized and demanded over and over, "Stop. You must stop." No one paid him any attention.

Finally Grove lay subdued and cursing on the ground. Fiona looked to see Constance standing white-faced and motionless.

"I don't understand," the younger woman said hollowly.

James went to her, put his arms around her, and murmured comforting words.

Fiona looked toward William. He looked wordlessly back at her. But a wealth of information was exchanged in that look. He did not look triumphant, only concerned at what she would think. He seemed to be imploring her not to think too ill of him because of this. As Fiona glanced again at her brother, she realized William could have taken the opportunity to kill Grove with the knife he had taken from him. He had not, and she knew that she was part of the reason why.

"It was such a shock," Constance said the next day as they stood in the parlor of the inn to which they had repaired after the incidents of the previous night. "How could Grove have been doing this all these years without being discovered?"

"Because he almost never stopped anyone so near the house," Fiona replied. "He ranged far from his home." She turned to look out the window of the parlor, hoping her sister would take the hint that she wanted to be alone. Fiona did not want to be unsociable, but at the moment she had no wish to further discuss the incidents of yesterday.

Constance, however, was still absorbed in the drama. Because she had never really known Grove, she viewed the whole situation more as an outsider. She did not feel the pain or hurt that Fiona felt. Besides, Constance had James to turn to for support.

Constance pulled back the curtains and looked out across the wide moors. "I shall be ever so glad when James returns with the special license. It is wonderful that you and William have given your approval. I am persuaded Mama will also give hers once she meets James. And once she learns the truth about what happened between William and Grove," Constance added.

"I do not know that she needs to hear the whole truth," Fiona said. It would pain Mama to learn her son was a thief. Still, she must be told that William did not shoot without warning during the duel.

"But if Grove goes to jail, Mama will have to learn the truth."

Fiona bit her lip. If Grove were sent to jail, it would kill Mama.

A knock sounded on the door. Constance opened it to find William Haversly standing on the threshold. "Is James with you?" she asked eagerly.

"No."

"Oh." Visibly disappointed, she excused herself to go in search of him.

That left Fiona and William alone together. Fiona

felt suddenly awkward and shy. "Please sit down." She knocked a teacup off as she gestured toward a chair. "How clumsy of me," she murmured and leaned forward to pick it up.

"Leave it, Fiona."

She straightened to look at him. "Have you news of Grove?"

"Yes. I spoke with the constable. Your brother has come under suspicion before, but nothing was ever proved against him. He seldom robbed people around here, but the temptation of seeing a solitary vehicle crossing the moor in the dark last night must have been too much for him."

"Is he being well taken care of? Was he cut badly?"

"The cut is deep," William confessed. "It is on his leg, so it does not pose a threat to his life. Still, the surgeon does not believe he will walk well again. He may be able to hobble, but that is the best to be hoped for."

She was silent. It was hard that her only brother should end up this way. She knew that the truth would be the death of her mother. "Will he go to jail?"

William sat down across from her. "That depends," he said slowly.

She waited.

"I am not without influence, Fiona. What do you want me to do about Grove?"

She swallowed hard. "I am grateful for your offer to help, but I am also at a loss to understand it. This is your chance to get revenge at Grove." Her throat constricted, but she forced herself to look at him and continue. "It is your chance to get revenge at me for treating you so shabbily. Yet you wish to be generous."

"I do not do this for Grove. I care nothing for him," he said bluntly. He moved closer so that she could see the deeper gray flecks around his gray irises. "I offer to help because of you. Even at our worst, there was always something between us. I think we both felt it the day of Eliza's funeral and again after Constance's party."

She nodded gravely. Yes, something had always remained between them in spite of her best efforts to root it out. But part of her had continued to care. Because he was on her mind more than she wanted to acknowledge, he had become a figure in her book. He had been a source of comfort to her on the wild trip out here to Cornwall.

"Tell me what you want," he said.

"Grove could be sent far away to another country. As a cripple, he would not be able to continue his criminal activities there." Her words were a breathless blur. Her thoughts were on his gaze and his declaration that he was doing all this because of her.

"I have thought of that. He could be sent to America or to Australia, perhaps."

She nodded. There was silence between them. She was swollen with emotion but words were difficult. "I—You said you were helping Grove because of me. You make me feel guilty because I have been unkind to you. I feel I should repay you somehow."

A slow smile worked at the corners of his mouth. "You will have a chance to do that in London."

What was he saying? "But I leave tomorrow to return to Surrey." It was difficult to maintain a conversation when he was so close to her, the warmth of his breath fluttering against her cheek. "Now that Constance's future is assured, I have no reason to go to London."

"I am a reason to go to London," he said simply.

She looked steadily at him. "Yes, you are."

"And not because you owe me a favor."

"I would not go because of that." The layers of tension that had separated them for years unraveled as she spoke. It was like talking with the William she had known as a debutante. "I would go to London because you ask me to and because I want to be with you."

He reached out to touch her face.

Quietly, she added, "You told me that you were in love with me nine years ago. I was in love with you then, too. Perhaps we can rekindle that feeling."

He smiled.

She smiled back at him. "I daresay I am being very bold, but I am too old to be coy or missish."

A teasing look came into his eyes. "Yes, at your advanced age, Fiona, you cannot wait long for the right man. I think you should take the first man to come along."

"I think so, too."

He bent forward to kiss her. Fiona thought it a fitting conclusion to the conversation, since words were no longer adequate to the task of conveying emotions. There was still much to be said, but it could be expressed better in kisses and touches and lingering looks. She relaxed into his arms. They had all the time in the world to continue this dialogue.

Regency...

HISTORICAL ROMANCE
AT ITS FINEST